the KIDNEY HYPOTHETICAL

or how to ruin your life in seven days

Lisa Yee

SCHOLASTIC INC.

This book is dedicated to Bean.

Copyright © 2015 by Lisa Yee

Arthur A. Levine Books hardcover edition designed by Elizabeth B. Parisi, published by Arthur A. Levine Books, an imprint of Scholastic Inc., April 2015.

All rights reserved. Published by Scholastic Inc., *Publishers since 1920*. SCHOLASTIC, the LANTERN LOGO, and associated logos are trademarks and/or registered trademarks of Scholastic Inc.

ISBN 978-0-545-23095-7

10 9 8 7 6 5 4 3 2 1   16 17 18 19 20

Printed in the U.S.A.   40
First printing 2016
Book design by Elizabeth B. Parisi

Sunday

Day 7

CHAPTER 1

I t was supposed to be the best week of my life, but then every-thing went terribly wrong. Actually, things had gone terribly wrong long before that, but no one had bothered to notice.

"I'm the king of the world!"

Kidding! Of course I was only kidding. That's a line from *Titanic*, a cheesy movie that makes girls go all soft because Leonardo DiCaprio dies in the film. That's right . . . Romance = Death.

I guess it's good that Leonardo died, because when a girl is sobbing, you can put your arm around her and tell her that you know how she feels. Then she thinks you're the sensitive type, when really, Leonardo drowning in freezing water isn't what's on your mind. The scene where Kate Winslet is naked is what you're really thinking about.

"Say it again, Higgs," Roo begged.

I stretched out my arms, leaned over the ship's rail, and yelled, "I'm king of the world!"

As Roo squealed, Nick tapped me on the shoulder and asked in his best English accent, which sounded more Brooklyn than British, "Pardon me, but are you quite done?" He adjusted the collar of his *Sgt. Pepper's Lonely Hearts Club* jacket — it was lime green, the color John Lennon wore. "I believe it's my turn."

Nick worshipped at the altar of John Lennon. He even had shaggy hair and wore round wire-rimmed glasses like his idol. I didn't have the heart to tell him that he looked more like a beefy, overgrown Harry Potter than an iconic musician from Liverpool.

Just then, I made the mistake of looking down into the bottomless ocean of blue-gray water. "Yeah, I'm done," I said quickly as we walked past the long line of seniors who had the same original idea as we did. "Come on, Roo, let's get out of here."

Roo was my girlfriend. She had that whole blond hair, blue-eyed, sun-kissed SoCal tan thing going for her. Not that I was complaining. Roo was one of the most beautiful girls at school. Everybody loved Roo. You'd have to be insane not to.

Sophomore year, Roo and I had been bio lab partners, then friends. No one was more surprised than me when we got together. Not known for her brains, I gave Roo gravitas and she gave me glamour. We'd been together for two years.

"Two years, four months, and seven days," she said as I tried not to vomit. I shouldn't have looked down from the bow of the ship. "Oh, Higgs, can you believe that we are going to graduate in six days? It's going to be the first day of the rest of our lives."

Either the ship was rocking violently or I was. "Every day is the first day of the rest of our lives," I told her as I wove my way to an empty table.

As Roo thought about this, I took a deep breath and stared at the centerpiece — a miniature life preserver with our school mascot, an astronaut, sitting in it.

Out of nowhere, Nick appeared and handed me a cold can of Coke. Good ol' Nick. He was always there for me. Unfortunately, Samantha Verve was at his side. "Who are you supposed to be?" I asked.

She was wearing a floppy white hat over her curly brown hair, a short white dress, and white boots, which matched the color of her skin. How anyone could live in Southern California and be so pale was a paradox.

Samantha lowered her oversized sunglasses. "I'm Yoko Ono," she said, as if it was something I should know.

"You broke up the Beatles," I said flatly. I wasn't sure if my nausea was getting worse because of the rocking ship or the proximity to Samantha Verve.

Samantha was Nick's girlfriend. No, wait. She was his fiancée. I'm serious. Fiancée.

Samantha proposed at prom, and Nick said yes.

And people thought *I* was crazy.

Roo leaned up against me. "This is nice, isn't it?" she asked.

I nodded stiffly. Her perfume was making my situation worse. I felt like I was suffocating, and it wasn't just that afternoon. I'd felt that way for two years, four months, and seven days. Still, so many people said Roo and I belonged together that I had talked myself into believing it. Actually, it was mostly Roo who said that, but everyone agreed with her. She had a way of getting people to do whatever she wanted, only making it seem like it was their idea.

When my brother, Jeffrey, was a senior, it was tradition to have a class picnic the Sunday before graduation. My senior year, the student council, led by Zander Findley, opted for a "Senior Sail," which meant that we were trapped on a ship that circled the Marina del Rey harbor for four hours. Everyone was encouraged to wear something that symbolized their years at Sally Ride High School. The football team wore their helmets, which made it hard for them to eat the little sandwiches the refreshment committee put out, French club members donned berets, and there was a group of kids wearing top hats and monocles, though I wasn't sure what that was supposed to mean. To be funny, Mr. Avis, the assistant principal, wore a prison guard uniform.

I wasn't sure how to dress — a suit for debate, my track uniform, or maybe the black shirt, red tie, and porkpie hat we wore for jazz band? I was also president of the honor society and valedictorian — what would symbolize that? I seriously considered wearing a Harvard T-shirt since my entire high school career had been focused on getting accepted there.

However, in the end, Roo insisted we dress as king and queen of the prom, which we were. That's how I ended up wearing a crown and sitting at a table with John Lennon and Yoko Ono as a ship sailed to nowhere while I tried not to throw up.

Day 7

CHAPTER 2

A re you really so sick that you can't dance?" Roo asked again.
"I am going to vomit," I said in a calm, measured voice.
Four years on the debate team, three of them varsity, taught me
that in times of crisis it was best to just communicate the facts
and leave emotion out of it.

"But you can still dance," she said, pouting. "Higgs, they're
playing our song."

The strains of Journey's "Don't Stop Believin'" were broadcast
over the tinny loudspeakers. As it went "on and on and on and
on," I looked up to see Samantha leading Nick to the dance floor.

"Higgs," Roo persisted, "this is our last Senior Sail."

"Roo, it's our only Senior Sail."

Just then Zander Findley materialized. We had been rivals
since forever. One of the benefits of dating Roo was knowing
that she was the girl of Zander's dreams.

"If you need someone who will dance with you, I'm here,"
he said.

Zander, who was prematurely mature, was in his usual garb — jeans, a turtleneck, and a brown corduroy jacket with patches at the elbows. His blow-dried hair had the hardened sheen of too much product, and he was one of the only kids at school with a serious mustache. He looked more like someone from his father's generation than ours.

"I'd love to dance with you," Roo said, glancing at me. "Higgs is being a party pooper."

"Higgs, do you mind?" Zander asked smugly as he extended his hand to Roo. He didn't wait for my answer.

As the boat rocked, I tried not to barf, which was difficult since my girlfriend and my enemy, neither great dancers, were boogying to ABBA's "Dancing Queen." Nearby, Nick and Samantha did the twist, as if they were listening to an entirely different song. At one point, Roo and Samantha began to waltz, while Nick continued to twist, leaving Zander dancing awkwardly by himself.

"Settle a bet," Samantha said to me after the song ended. She had a dangerous smile on her face.

"I'm telling you, I won this," Roo giggled.

"Higgs, if Roo needed a kidney, would you give her one of yours?"

It seemed like a straightforward question, but I should have guessed that coming from Samantha Verve, it was a trap.

"I'm not going to answer that," I said. "Roo's kidneys are fine and I'm not into hypotheticals."

I couldn't believe we were even having this conversation.

Samantha wouldn't let go. "So that means no, then?"

"I didn't say that."

"But you didn't say yes," Samantha said, glancing triumphantly at Roo.

Roo cast her gaze toward the ocean. The sun was starting to set.

"Would you give Roo one of your kidneys if she needed one?" Samantha asked again.

"Why? Why are we even discussing this?" I cried, restraining my urge to throw up. "Christ, Samantha, drop it. What is your problem?"

"I would give you one of mine," Roo said softly. Her eyes were moist.

"Roo, don't let her do this to us," I said. It wasn't the first time Samantha tried to break us up.

Samantha turned to Nick. "If I needed a kidney, would you give me one of yours?"

Nick's eyes met mine.

"Don't look at him, look at me," Samantha ordered. "Would you give me a kidney?"

"Well, sure," he said, still staring at me. He mouthed, "I'm sorry."

"You don't love me!" Roo cried.

"Roo . . . ," I started to say. "I . . ."

"If you loved me, you would give me a kidney," she wailed.

"I'm not even going to discuss this anymore. It's a hypothetical!" I said, glaring at Samantha. The conversation was making me even more nauseated than I already was.

"It's over, then," Roo said, sounding small.

"Well, thank god for that," I answered. The topic was stupid. Samantha Verve was stupid. The conversation was stupid.

"Thank god?" Roo echoed. "Thank god that our relationship is over?"

"Wha . . . ? No, I thought you were talking about the kidney thing —"

"It doesn't matter. You've ruined my life!" Roo shouted as she raised her hands to the sky. She was in the drama club and they were all like that. "Higgs Boson Bing, you are heartless. I could have died without your kidney."

"I'd give you both my kidneys and my heart," Zander said.

I couldn't hold back any longer.

"HIGGS!" Roo shrieked.

"Gotta go!" Zander said, quickly retreating.

It probably wasn't a good time to throw up, but then is there ever a good time for that?

Nick was trying not to laugh, and even from behind her dark glasses, I could tell that Samantha was glaring at me. Roo stood frozen with her hands clenched and her face screwed up as if she had just seen her boyfriend barf on her.

"I'm sorry," I told her. "I'll pay for your dress."

Even though I had made a mess, I felt so much better. Funny, isn't it? You hold back, and you hold back, because you don't want to cause a scene, but when you finally let go, it can be a relief. A mess, but a relief.

"Arrrggggg!!!!" Roo screamed. "I hate you, Higgs Boson Bing!"

As if things couldn't get worse, Rosalee Gomez strolled over. Rosalee was always the first to try to cut me down. We were both in speech and debate, but have never been on the same team.

"Nice one, Bing," Rosalee said. She adjusted her beret and then pointed to my mess on the floor. "Let me guess . . . nachos?"

"Right again, Rosalee," I said. "Help yourself. You're always up for a free meal."

Gossip spreads fast in high school. I would say that it spreads like wildfire, but that wouldn't be right. It spreads faster. There's nothing more invigorating to the student body than a good rumor, especially if it's about someone you know.

As a disgruntled ship employee was dispatched to get a mop, several guys who were actually drunk gave me the thumbs-up. "Higgs was so drunk he puked," I heard people saying, not unkindly.

"What just happened?" I asked.

The crowd parted as Samantha and a gaggle of other girls escorted a sobbing Roo to the bathroom. "He doesn't love me," she could be heard telling startled onlookers. "I could have died."

"Whose nightmare am I in?" I asked. "Why is this happening?"

Nick shook his head and answered, "You should have given her a kidney."

Day 7

CHAPTER 3

The ship still had an hour and a half of circling the harbor before docking, which meant that I had an hour and a half of avoiding Roo. I considered jumping and swimming to shore, but with one week before graduation I figured it was best not to court trouble.

"Maybe you can just say you were wrong and beg for forgiveness," Nick said. He cleaned his glasses on the sleeve of his jacket. "That always works for me."

The strange thing was, I wasn't sure if I wanted Roo back.

You'd think that after being in a relationship with someone for over two years, one ought to have felt some remorse. But oddly, I didn't. And when I really thought about it, I wasn't even sure why we were together to begin with. Oh sure, we had a lot of fun. And as I've noted before, Roo was gorgeous, but it was not without a price. I probably spent one entire year of our relationship waiting for her to get ready. Still, anyone would be proud to have Roo for a girlfriend, and I don't deny that being with her raised my status immensely at school. But let's face it, Roo was clingy.

The upside of dating Roo was that it gave Nick and me a good excuse to hang out together. Before Roo, it was always Nick and me, and Samantha. Although to hear her tell it, it was Nick and Samantha, and me. Samantha Verve and Roo were best friends and when we double-dated, the guys sat in the front of the car and the girls were in the back. Lots of times I just pretended they weren't even there. I wished I could do that now, but instead I was trapped on the Senior Sail version of the *Titanic*, and we know how that ended.

Nick and I were hiding out in the far corner of the dance floor, watching some of the soccer guys play air guitar, when I spotted it.

"Holy shit," I said.

Nick looked up. "Holy shit," he said.

We both took a couple of steps backward and hit a wall.

A clump of angry girls was striding toward us. In the center was Roo. I swear, at that very moment the DJ started playing "Eye of the Tiger" by Survivor and the girls moved as if in slow motion — angry slow motion — and headed straight toward us.

Samantha Verve, the only person Nick has ever truly feared, got to me first. "You're scum! Look what you did," she shouted, pointing. I looked at my ex-girlfriend, and when someone nudged her, she turned on the tears. Roo's timing, or rather lack of it, during school plays was legendary. "You denied her a life-saving kidney, and then you threw up on her!"

"It's your fault she's crying," I told Samantha. "You and your kidney hypothetical. If Roo is going to be upset at someone, it should be you. You set this up and you know it."

"Oh! Oh, you . . . Oh! Oh! Oh!" Samantha replied, which is exactly the sort of nonstatement I'd come to expect from her.

I could not understand how or why someone as smart as Nick could be in love with Samantha. She must have put a hex on him.

"Having trouble with those pesky nouns and verbs again, Samantha?" I asked.

Then, probably because she had always enjoyed being the star of her own drama, Roo gave the performance of her life. She sobbed louder than the lead singer shrieking in the chorus of "Eye of the Tiger," which in itself was impressive.

"You poo!" Roo shouted, exiting stage left with her Greek chorus murmuring "he's a poo" and "poor Roo" and "heartless" as they trailed their Antigone.

"Hey Higgs," a football player called out, "score one for Team Roo!"

"Pity she dumped you," someone else said.

I turned around to find Zander Findley smirking. "What do you want, Zander?"

"From you? Nothing. Oh, wait. You know a bunch of us are taking bets, you want in?"

My eyes narrowed. I've never trusted Zander. "Bets about what?" I asked.

"On how big an asshole you are. I say you're number one."

"No, that would be you, Zander."

"I didn't break poor Roo's heart," he said, flicking a piece of cracker off his sleeve.

"I didn't break her heart," I corrected him. "I just didn't give her a kidney."

"A true gentleman would have offered her one. As it was, I offered her two," he said.

"You're an idiot," I muttered.

I hated it that people sometimes confused us.

Zander was a white Anglo-Saxon Protestant with a ridiculously chiseled chin that looked like plastic surgery run amok. I was of mixed race (Chinese/English), though my father would say that I slightly favored my Asian side, and my mother would say the opposite. My hair was black, my eyes were brown, I stood six feet even, and I had a strong but lanky build. Old ladies often told me that I had a charming smile.

HIGGS	ZANDER
Debate Team Captain	*Academic Decath Co-Captain*
Prom King	*Homecoming King*
Track Team (high jump)	*Golf*
Co-Valedictorian	*Co-Valedictorian*
Honor Society President	*Senior Council President*
Early Admissions: Harvard	*Early Admissions: Princeton*
Jazz Band: Alto Sax	*Band: Drum Line*
Girlfriend: Rosemary "Roo" Wynn	*Girlfriend: None*
The Proclamation *Newspaper*	Reflections/snoitcelfeR *Yearbook*
Boys State Representative	*Exchange Student (Madrid)*

Zander Findley and I were pretty much tied in terms of who ruled the school. However, the upcoming Senior of the Year award would decide that once and for all. Not to leave anything to chance, on Saturday, Nick and I had plastered "Higgs for Senior of the Year" flyers all over campus. The rationale was that on Monday, the selection committee members — no one knew who they were — would see them and be reminded of me when the votes were cast.

"Well, sorry about your girlfriend," Zander said, not looking sorry at all. "I'd love to stay and chat, but I'm bored."

"Likewise, I am sure," I said, yawning broadly.

"Oh, and Higgs," Zander said, "your crown is crooked. Or should I say c-c-c-crooked?"

I winced, but only for a second.

"Shove it, Zander," I said. "You won't be so happy when I get Senior of the Year."

"Ah, but that's not going to happen, is it?" he said ominously.

My anger rose as I watched him walk away. I could have destroyed him right then and there. However, if I did, he could have done the same to me. We knew each other too well.

"I'm going to find Samantha," Nick announced.

I had forgotten he was there. From the moment he and Samantha set eyes on each other in freshman Honors English, they had been in love, or so they claimed. I'm not sure I know what being in love is.

When I was little, I asked my dad what love is and he was silent for so long that I thought he hadn't heard me. Finally, he said, "Love means taking out the trash before you are told to."

When I asked my mom what love is, she glanced at Dad, then said, "Love is overlooking the flaws."

So if that's love, I didn't need it.

I dunno. Maybe if Leonardo had hung on to his own life instead of trying to save Kate Winslet, he wouldn't have drowned.

Day 7

CHAPTER 4

Roo was playing the part of the innocent victim to the hilt, repeating the story each time someone new showed up. ". . . he refused to give me a kidney, and when I asked again, he threw up on me!"

I couldn't pass a girl without getting glared at, that's how quickly the kidney hypothetical had gotten around. If it weren't for Nick, there's no way I would have survived the rest of the Senior Sail. He was my lookout, and whenever he spied Roo, who was on the rampage, he steered me away from her.

"Pizza?" I asked as the ship neared shore. My appetite had suddenly reappeared and I was famished.

Nick shook his head. "Señor Carlos."

Oh, right. Señor Carlos. The four of us had planned on having dinner there. It was our usual place. Great food. Cheap. "You're still going?" I asked.

"Well, yeah," Nick said. "You and Roo may have broken up, but that doesn't mean that Samantha and I have too."

I don't know why that surprised me, but it did.

When I got home, my mother was talking to Jeffrey. She was always talking to Jeffrey. "Can you believe that your little brother is graduating from high school soon?" she asked. When he didn't answer, Mom continued, "It didn't seem like so long ago that you were graduating. . . ." Her voice trailed off.

"Hey, Higgs," my father called out from his leather armchair. Golf was on the television and the sportscasters were whispering even though they were nowhere near the tee.

Dad held up an empty glass. I added four fresh ice cubes, before pouring the Chivas, and handed his beloved Scotch on the rocks back to him. I didn't know how he could drink that stuff, especially because of what had happened. After the accident, it seemed like my father picked up his pace as if to make up for my mother, who had stopped drinking alcohol entirely.

"What are you doing home?" Mom asked.

She gazed at the oversized portrait of my brother in his high school graduation cap and gown, his good looks and effortless smile forever beaming down on us. Below it, on the fireplace mantle, was the Jeffrey Arthur Bing shrine — trophies, high school diploma, baby shoes; it was all there.

Even though it had been years since my brother died, my parents still talked to him. In fact, they talked to him more than they talked to each other.

"I just wanted to be with you guys," I said. "What's for dinner?"

"Oh, Higgs . . ." Mom's voice cracked. "I am going to miss you so much when you leave. We're going to be all alone here."

"So nice to know how much I'm loved," my sister said as she slumped into the room. Her wardrobe consisted of ratty jeans, ratty Converse, and ratty, yet expensive, T-shirts designed to convey the message of rebel youth with an artistic bent. She hung out with the artsy crowd, who took great pains perfecting the I-don't-care look.

"You know we love you." Mom stared at my brother's portrait as she hugged my sister. "It's just that Higgs is —"

"We all know what he is," my sister said, pulling away. "He's *the* Higgs Boson, the God particle, the missing link, the answer to all the questions of the universe."

"Drop it, Charlie," my father said without taking his eyes off the television.

Charlie. That's my sister's name.

Maybe I'd better explain. My father's full name is Charles Arthur Bing. My great-great-great-grandfather, Ah Bing, invented the Bing cherry when he lived in Oregon. Later, he was deported back to China under the Chinese Exclusion Act of 1882. So, yes, that cherry pie so many Americans enjoy every Fourth of July was courtesy of a deported immigrant.

My mother was an immigrant too, though no one has ever attempted to throw her out of the country, probably because she has a refined accent. Mom hailed from Stratford-upon-Avon, the birthplace of William Shakespeare. Strangers often mentioned her resemblance to the actress Kristin Scott Thomas, who starred in the movie *The English Patient* alongside Voldemort, or at least the actor who played him. Despite her having lived in America for most of her life, Mom still spoke as if she were ordering high tea on the Thames. Her name is Elizabeth Mary Barrington Clarke Cooper Miller, and she is three-quarters Jewish. My mother kept her maiden name. All of them.

The Asian Jewish English American thing was a real stumper when it came to filling out my college applications. In Ivy League circles, being an overachieving Asian was actually a detriment, and it was rumored that colleges had a secret quota. Being Jewish was of little help since it didn't qualify me as a minority. In the end, my college coach suggested we list me as "other."

Mom had a BA in astronomy and a master's in astrophysics. She was working on her PhD at the time of the accident and was a respected scientist at NASA's Jet Propulsion Lab, a couple of miles from our house. It was her idea to name me Higgs Boson, after the elusive particle. Dad wanted to name me Charles.

"But he'll already be named after you — his last name will be Bing," my mother countered.

The compromise was that the next child would be named after my father, which is how my little sister came to be called Charles Louise Bing, a.k.a. Charlie. Ever since she found out that Charles was supposed to be my name, she's been pissed at me — which means that she has been pissed at me for most of her life.

Charlie was a freshman and got good grades, which was mandatory in my family. Yet she acted like she didn't care. She was a straight-A slacker. My sister didn't do much, unless you counted slouching around the house or stinking up her room with paint and art supplies. Every so often, she'd go off on some rant about artists being underappreciated and persecuted. When that happened, we'd just ignore her.

A commercial for the new courtroom TV series *Annie McAndrews, Esq.* came on. "She's got beautiful teeth," Dad said.

He ought to know. My father was "Dr. Charles Bing, the

painless dentist." With his athlete's build, thick black hair, and magnetic smile, Dad was so handsome that everyone — men, women, babies, dogs — stared at him. He could have been in *Charles Bing, DDS* if there was such a thing as a Chinese American television star who was not skilled in martial arts. However, it didn't matter that he couldn't break bricks with his bare hands. In the Bing family, we brandished our awards and diplomas like weapons.

I had never seen my father happier than the day I got into Harvard. He kept telling me how proud he was that I was carrying on the family tradition. I was on track to be the third Dr. Bing, DDS, my grandfather being the first. It made me feel great that Dad felt so great.

"So then," my father said as he changed the channel and landed on CNN. It looked like there was a revolution going on, but I couldn't tell where since the TV was now on mute. "Martin Gowin, you know, the lawyer from Rotary, has a daughter your age."

Why was he telling me this? I wondered.

"She's in France right now on a student exchange program," Dad explained as buildings burned on TV. "She goes to Our Lady of the Holy Cross Excelsior Academy and will be attending Tufts in the fall, and then the plan is on to Yale for law school. Tufts isn't too far from Harvard. Maybe when you're there you could visit her. That way you'll both know someone from home."

As if on cue, a television commercial for Gowin, Gowin, Gowin & Gowin came on. "Go win with Gowin!" the lawyers said as they turned and pointed to the camera in unison. I wondered how many takes it took them to get it right.

"Great slogan," Dad noted. "Martin's the second from the left. So, what do you think Higgs? It wouldn't hurt you to be nice to her."

"What would Roo think of that?" my mother asked.

"Roo might be glad to be rid of Higgs," Charlie volunteered.

I had no desire to befriend a shy future lawyer from Gowin, Gowin, Gowin & Gowin. "May I be excused?" I asked as I headed outside.

"You always are, Farmer Higgs," Charlie quipped as I walked past her. "Be sure to check on your dingleberries."

"Dingleberries — what's that?" Mom asked.

"Just something Higgs grows in his garden," Charlie said, laughing at her own joke.

My tomatoes were doing well. The cucumbers were getting big too. And the strawberries were as red and ripe as I had ever seen them. The plot of land had been used for Jeffrey's batting practice. After he died, Mom couldn't stand the sight of it, so she planted an English vegetable garden like the one her grandmother had back home. It was one of many hobbies my mother attempted to fill her days with. She also went though a bread machine phase, collected ceramic owls, and took Bikram Yoga — but didn't even make it through the first class. "I don't like to perspire in public," she explained. "It's undignified."

The garden was different, though. It proved to be surprisingly therapeutic and had staying power. Not for my mother, but for me.

Day 7

CHAPTER 5

That night, I couldn't sleep. All I could think about was Roo and the whole kidney hypothetical. I felt so guilty. Not about refusing to hand over a kidney, and not that we had broken up over a hypothetical — but rather, I felt guilty that I didn't feel guilty.

The truth was that for months I had wanted to break up with Roo. Once you got over how gorgeous she was, there really wasn't much "there" there. Roo always got the starring roles in our school plays based on her looks, not her talent, she was a less than stellar student, and she refused to read Kurt Vonnegut. I couldn't see us being together while I was at Harvard.

Long-distance relationships rarely work out. We had seen *Still Friends*, that movie about a high school couple who tried to stay together while going to college on separate coasts. Being apart caused them to question their love for each other, and in the end, the guy committed suicide by riding his horse off a cliff. I thought the movie was prophetic and I worried about the horse. Roo thought it was romantic.

Even though it was late, there was a knock on my bedroom door. Mom. My heart sank when I saw that she was wearing the fluffy pink bathrobe that Charlie had nicknamed the "Robe of Depression."

"I saw your light on," my mother said. She wandered around my room and ran her fingertips across a framed photo of me, Charlie, and Jeffrey standing in front of the Christmas tree. I was nine, Charlie was five, and Jeffrey was eighteen.

"Well," Mom said, absentmindedly picking up a *Top Cop* baseball cap and putting it on. It had belonged to my brother. *Top Cop* was his all-time favorite television show. He was obsessed with cops. No one was allowed to talk to him when it was on. "I just wanted to remind you to make sure that Roo's parents know they are invited to your graduation party."

I nodded. There was no way I was going to tell my mother about Roo when she was wearing that bathrobe.

My mother had been acting weirder than normal lately, and she moved around as if in a fog of forgetfulness. For example, she'd be standing in the living room holding a pair of scissors and saying, "Why am I holding these?" Then there was the crying. Mom would cry over things like when the cottage cheese expired, or when a down-on-his-luck singer won a TV talent show. Or when she thought about my brother. She cried about him the most.

My mother sat on the edge of my bed and stared at me in that mom way. "Oh, Higgs, you're going to graduate soon. It's so hard to believe. I remember when you were just starting kindergarten, and now look at you."

When she began to weep, I gave her a hug. "Everything's going to be all right," I told her.

She wiped her eyes with the sleeve of her robe. "That's what your father always says," she told me. She sounded bitter. "Higgs?"

"Yes?"

"You're just like him. You know that, don't you?"

"Like Dad?"

She winced, then shook her head. "Please, no, not your father. Like Jeffrey. You're like Jeffrey. Handsome. Top of your class. Going to Harvard. You be careful, okay?"

"I'll be careful," I promised her.

She kissed me on the forehead and got up to leave.

"Um, Mom?"

"Yes?"

"The baseball cap." I motioned to her head.

"Of course," she said, giving it to me. "What was I thinking?"

It was past midnight. I put on some John Lennon. Nick would have approved. Good old Nick Milgram. In elementary school, we ate lunch together every day, we both belonged to Cub Scout Pack #475, and we shared a bunk at Camp Cougar Mountain, which had neither cougars nor a mountain.

In middle school, Nick and I excelled in student activities, honors classes, and music. Slowly, we went from invisible to center stage. Whereas in elementary school we admired the popular kids, in middle school we became them. In sixth grade, we were on honor patrol. In seventh, we were both on student council. In eighth grade, I was class president and Nick was vice president.

Like my brother, I started playing alto sax in the fifth grade. When Nick first started band, he was a 70-pound weakling and could barely lift his tuba. While others might have given up, Nick stuck with it. Several years and 110 pounds later, he would

23

be realizing his dream and marching in the USC Trojan Band this fall.

Samantha was going to USC too, which surprised me. I didn't think she had the grades, but apparently she aced her SAT. Nick and Samantha only applied to the same colleges. Roo was going to DePaul University to major in theater.

"You know what's going to happen, don't you?" I had told Nick when we were writing our college essays. "You and Samantha are going to get in a huge fight right before finals, and then both of you will fail and have to drop out of school."

Without taking his eyes off his laptop, Nick slapped me in the head. "You're such a prick, Higgs," he said.

I was going to miss Nick. Now that Roo was out of my life, I thought that maybe I could talk him into ditching Samantha and we could hang out. Without Roo, I was going to have so much free time that summer. I could graft those peaches in my garden, and I could set up a stall at the farmer's market. I could finish reading *Breakfast of Champions*, and even date other girls, something I hadn't done in years. I could do whatever I wanted.

Yes, a Roo-less summer was going to be a great thing.

The more I thought about it, the better my world looked. Shoot. I was going to Harvard. I should have been proud of that, right? Thirty-five thousand applicants and only 6 percent got in. All that I had left to do was to slide through the last week of school. Everyone knew that for seniors, it was like a vacation. And there was Senior of the Year too. I was looking forward to accepting that award.

It was funny. Earlier in the day, I was distraught over my breakup with Roo, but after carefully thinking things through, I was certain that I was heading into the best week of my life.

Monday

Day 6

CHAPTER 6

Charlie slept in on Monday morning, which was unlike her. As rebellious as she liked to appear, my little sister prided herself on being punctual. Then again, the last week of school made kids do strange things. Same for the teachers — some of them actually smiled. With tests done, grades in, and the promise of summer beckoning, everyone let their guard down. It was liberating.

My last four years had been rough. On the outside, it looked like I had breezed my way to a 4.35 GPA. In reality, I worked my ass off. Unlike my brother, or Nick, I was not a genius. But I'd be damned if I let anyone know that, especially someone like Zander Findley, who would have mocked me unmercifully had he known the truth.

At home, I'd blast the music in my room, then put on noise-canceling headphones and dive into my books. I found no joy in studying, and getting high grades wasn't so much a reward, but a relief at not having failed. You know what they say, "school,

27

sleep, or socialize — pick two"? Thank god for coffee and NoDoz.

Usually, Charlie was the one who made sure I was awake in the morning, and did so by shouting and hitting me over the head with a pillow until I got up. I suspected that she enjoyed this much more than she let on. My parents insisted I drive my sister to school. It was part of the bargain when they bought me a car. The caveat was that Charlie would inherit it when I went away to Harvard. Neither one of us was too keen on the make and model, though.

"Volvo station wagons are the safest cars on the road," my mother said.

"Does it have to be red?" I moaned. "It looks like a fire truck."

"Precisely," she answered. "People will give you a wide berth."

I knew not to press the issue.

That day, when I awoke to my alarm clock instead of my sister, a strange sensation washed over me. It was as if I had finally managed to break free of Roo and surface after being held underwater.

Mom was talking to Jeffrey and wearing her pink Robe of Depression, so I knew to avoid her. She had been wearing the robe more and more lately. Dad saw her standing in front of my brother's photo yesterday and said, "Liz, maybe you ought to join a club or a gym or something. That might make you feel better. Isn't that right, Jeffrey?"

"I am just fine," she told him testily. "Maybe you ought to trying coming home at a decent hour."

Unlike my parents, I hardly ever spoke to Jeffrey. However, on the day I learned Harvard granted me an early admission, I stood in front of his portrait and told him, "I did it. I know you couldn't go, so I'll go for the both of us."

The only one in our family who didn't talk to Jeffrey was Charlie. She was so young when he died that she didn't know what it was like to have a big brother you loved more than anything, and who loved you back unconditionally.

After breakfast I ventured into my sister's room. Every inch of wall was covered with artsy-fartsy black-and-white photos ripped out of magazines. Her bookshelves were crammed with art books and worn black Moleskine notebooks filled with her weird drawings. One shelf was devoted to small plastic Japanese monsters that, inexplicably, looked adorable and terrifying at the same time. Charlie had safety-pinned old T-shirts together to create curtains, giving the room a laundry-clothesline effect. The only thing that seemed out of place was her Disney princesses bedspread.

I picked up a pillow and raised it above my head, ready to hit her. But my perpetually angry sister actually looked serene. I set the pillow down. "Charlie," I said, shaking her gently. "We're going to be late for school."

"I don't care," she murmured. "Go away, Higgs. Go away."

She rolled over and hugged Bunchy Bear. That was the only thing of Jeffrey's she had. As I looked at Charlie, my heart ached. Was it possible that I was going to miss my brat of a little sister? I wondered.

That's when I noticed all the dead plants on her windowsill. Plants I had given to her.

"CHARLIE!" I shouted. "You killed them!"

"Leave me alone," she muttered, pulling the sheets over her head.

"You have to water the plants," I continued yelling as I examined the dead dieffenbachia. Its broad, waxy green-and-white leaves had shriveled up and turned brown. It was nearly impossible to kill one of those, yet she did it. Next to it was a potted hibiscus — dead. A hedgehog cactus — dead. How the hell does one kill a cactus?

"You think they're just going to take care of themselves?"

"Go away, Farmer Higgs," she said, her eyes still shut. "They're just plants!"

Just plants? They weren't just plants. I nurtured and grew those, just like my garden in the backyard. Even though I won almost every award in high school, the one I was most proud of was the gold medal my peaches won at the L.A. County Fair.

"You're on your own, Charlie," I yelled before storming out of the house.

For the first time that year, I drove to school without my sister. It was weird not having her in the car criticizing me and my driving. A rusted green Kia was in my usual spot and the lot was full, so I was forced to find street parking — not an easy task when you drive a car as big as mine. I walked past a gang of dropouts who hung out across the street, got stoned, and mocked anyone who carried a backpack. If they hated high school enough to leave, then why did they still hang around?

One of them laughed when he saw me and handed me a flyer. I didn't even bother to read it. As I passed the old green car, I looked through the open window. Inside was littered with garbage. I crumpled up the flyer and tossed it into the Kia. What was one more piece of trash?

It felt good to be walking onto campus. It was my place. Our school was fairly new and visitors often mistook it for a college. In stark contrast, on top of the hill, the old water tower loomed over Sally Ride High School. It no longer serviced the town of Monte Vista, CA, but preservationists, my father among them, were in a constant battle to keep it from being torn down. They insisted that it was a symbol. A symbol for what, I could never figure out.

"Hi, Higgs!"

"Hey, it's the prom king!"

I'm not going to lie. It felt great to be popular. I smiled and nodded as I strolled down the hallway. With each greeting, I felt better. Maybe there wouldn't be any fallout from the kidney hypothetical after all.

"Hi, Higgs!"

"Hey, Higgs!"

"Fart sniffer."

I stopped. "Excuse me?" I said to Samantha.

"You heard me," she said. She was no longer dressed as Yoko Ono. Instead, she was wearing her private school uniform — navy skirt, white shirt, knee-high socks, and red Doc Martens. This was Samantha's way of being a rebel since we went to a public school. "Fart sniffer. Higgs, you are a fart sniffer and a horrible human being."

I really didn't have time for that. Clearly, Samantha was holding a Roo grudge. "Thank you, Samantha," I told her. "How is fourth grade going for you?"

I didn't wait for her reply. Instead, I continued toward the main gates and tried to shake off her rudeness. Still, my thoughts kept turning to Roo. I hoped she was okay. I mean, you don't date someone for two years, four months, and seven days and not feel a thing when you break up.

I unrolled a "Higgs Boson Bing for Senior of the Year" poster and taped it to the gate to go with the flyers that Nick and I had put up on Saturday. I knew it was overkill, but I wanted to be certain I would snag the award. It was the one accolade left for me to achieve in my high school career. Get that one, and I'd be the first student since the great Jeffrey Bing to sweep all the major awards.

Everyone said I was going to win — either me or Zander. We had both won so many things it was as if we were getting awards for getting awards.

As I entered campus, people stopped and stared. Some snickered. Maybe they had heard about Roo and me? I knew there would be rumors about our breakup and the barfing. I would have thought the vomiting on your girlfriend was the worse of the two evils, but apparently I was wrong. The kidney hypothetical was all everyone was talking about on the Senior Sail.

As I made my way down the hallway, more kids broke out grinning at the sight of me. Some held up their hands for a high five, which I gave them. "Thank you," I said each time. I wondered if Senior of the Year had been announced early. Maybe I didn't even need the flyers or posters. I was feeling nostalgic about high school and I hadn't even left yet. That is, until I rounded the corner and came to a dead stop.

I couldn't believe it.

I ripped the flyer off the wall and stared. There were dozens of them. In place of the "Higgs for Senior of the Year" flyers, someone had taken my graduation photo, the one where I look like Dean Cain, the actor who played the lead in the retro TV series *The New Adventures of Superman*, and defaced it. I now had a Hitler mustache, horns, and a gap-toothed smile.

That's when I noticed a bunch of freshmen laughing. I shoved a geek in the chest. "You think that's funny?" I asked.

The boy looked frightened, like he was going to pee. "N-no, sir. Higgs, sir," he stammered.

When he screwed his eyes shut, I noticed that my fist was in his face. I let him go and he ran down the hall, tripping as his friends scurried after him, laughing.

This couldn't be happening.

I raced along the corridor, tearing down the offending papers. Not a single "Higgs for Senior of the Year" was in evidence. Instead, the Hitler Higgs flyers lined the hallways.

Why? Why? Why?

The bell rang and the hallways emptied, except for me holding two fistfuls of wadded-up flyers with me looking like Hitler and a headline screaming "Higgs for Dinky Dick of the Year."

Day 6

CHAPTER 7

"Hi, Higgs."

Mrs. Sanchez's presence calmed me down, if only temporarily. Her gray hair was worn in a thick braid that went halfway down her back, and her smile radiated warmth even though the office thermostat must have been set to Arctic.

As the admin office manager, nothing got past Mrs. Sanchez. "Principal Kostantino's on an important call," she told me. "You can wait outside her office if you want."

I took a seat in the wobbly orange plastic chair, but got up to help Mrs. Sanchez when she tried to carry a big box of copier paper. She was small, like my mom.

The clock said I'd only been waiting for eight minutes, but it felt like forever. Clutching a fistful of flyers, I began pacing.

"Higgs, Principal Kostantino's going to be a while. What about Mr. Avis?" Mrs. Sanchez finally asked. She'd always been nice to me. Mrs. Sanchez used to work at the elementary school, and when I was going through my really bad time, she helped get me through it. There were numerous days when I just couldn't be in class, but didn't want to go home. So Mrs. Sanchez would let me sit next to her and staple papers or do other busywork.

"Fine," I said, even though everyone knew that Mr. Avis, the assistant principal, was basically ineffectual. Last year, there was a petition to get him fired after he had the sodas in the vending machines replaced with juice bottles and water. But a Mr. Avis was better than no one, and this couldn't wait.

"Ah, Mr. Bing," Mr. Avis said as I entered his office. The walls were lined with photos of him shaking hands with self-important–looking people I didn't recognize. "It looks like you've recovered from your vomitfest at the Senior Sail. I hope you won't be drinking at graduation."

I wanted to tell him that I didn't drink, but it wasn't worth wasting my breath. He would have thought I was lying. People believe what they want to believe.

"Mr. Avis," I said, still standing. He was a big man with comically broad shoulders, making his head look unusually small, like they ran out of the proper parts at the factory.

"How may I help you, Mr. Bing?"

"These!" I said, dumping the flyers on his desk. "They're all over school!"

He uncrumpled one. "Nice photo," he said wryly.

"Mr. Avis," I said, finding it increasingly more difficult to tamp down my anger, "this is slander and I demand that the school do something about it!"

"You demand the school do something about it?"

It was like talking to a parrot.

"Yes," I said. "I could sue the school."

35

"You could sue the school?" he said.

I shook my head. "For defamation of character!"

"For defamation of character? Sit down, Mr. Bing. Cool your jets."

He leaned back in his chair. I hoped it would tip over.

After staring at me for an uncomfortable amount of time, Mr. Avis spoke. "I will ask Mr. French, our custodial engineer, to take down the flyers. However, he and the rest of us are busy getting ready for Saturday's graduation ceremony." Mr. Avis paused as he pressed the tips of his fingers together and locked his eyes on me. "Do you have enemies, Mr. Bing?" he asked.

I shook my head. "No," I told him. "No enemies."

"No enemies? That surprises me. Clearly at least one person doesn't care for you. Is there anyone you've offended recently?"

"No. No one I can think of," I answered.

"No one?" Mr. Avis said. "You didn't, say, start any petitions to try to get rid of them or anything?"

He was baiting me, and we both knew it. So maybe I did sign the petition to get him fired, but I wasn't alone. Zander Findley and some of the other drum-line guys started it, yet I was the one who Mr. Avis has always blamed. He was too wrapped up in himself to see the truth.

"No petitions," I said, tight-lipped.

"Think hard, Mr. Bing," he said. "Students, teachers, staff, administration, surely among them, there must be someone who thinks that you are a spoiled, arrogant, entitled weasel —"

"Thank you, Mr. Avis," I said as I stood. "I'll be leaving now."

"Keep your eyes on your friends, Mr. Bing," he said as I left his office. "They could be your enemies."

Day 6

CHAPTER 8

The rest of the morning was hell disguised as high school. Apparently word had spread beyond the senior class that my incredible selfishness caused Roo and me to split up. Girls I didn't even know came up to me and said, "I can't believe you did that!" Or "You are so mean, she could have died!"

I finally gave up trying to explain that the kidney thing was a hypothetical. No one listened to me anyway since it made a better story to believe that I was the cause of Roo's imminent death. Couple that with the flyers and it was fair to say I was miserable. I couldn't wait for lunchtime so I could talk to Nick.

Seniors were allowed to eat off campus. It was a privilege granted to those of us who had managed to survive three years of the school cafeteria. When Nick and I walked into Benny's B-Burgers, I spotted Roo and Samantha, sitting in a corner booth. Both stopped talking when they saw me.

Nick made a beeline to Samantha, leaving me unprotected. I considered running away, but stood my ground even though

Roo was bombarding me with evil, stabbing glares, which I unsuccessfully tried to deflect by feigning interest in the Heimlich maneuver poster.

It was Samantha who encouraged Roo to go out with me. Back when I was a sophomore, I would have never asked Roo out on my own. I thought she was out of my league. Roo said I wasn't like the other guys who were jerks. She said I was stable, and she liked that I could help her with her homework, plus she said that we made a good-looking couple.

When Nick returned, he looked grave. "It's not safe for you to be here," he said, ushering me to the door.

As we ate our pepperoni pizza, Nick wiped some sauce off his chin. He had always been a messy eater. "I have no idea," he said when I offered up my theories on the flyers.

Every time someone called me Dinky Dick, I cringed. How do you defend yourself from something like that? In debate, we offer evidence. Proof. However, I wasn't about to do that in this case.

"Hey, Higgs," Nick said abruptly. "Samantha doesn't want me hanging out with you anymore."

"What?" I took a swig of Coke. "She said that?"

He nodded as he chewed slowly. "Samantha says that you hurt Roo, and that Roo is her best friend, and that your moral compass is broken."

My moral compass? I didn't even know I had one. I started to laugh.

"Seriously," Nick said, reaching for his third slice. "I can't hang out with you until this whole Roo kidney thing blows over."

I shook my head. "I can't even believe we're having this conversation!" Nick motioned to some girls from my Spanish class glaring at me from the next table. I waved to them. "*¿Qué pasa?*" I said before turning back to Nick and lowering my voice. "You're letting Samantha tell you who you can be friends with? What kind of wimp are you?"

"I'm a wimp in love," he said in all seriousness. "Listen, I take my cues from my old lady."

I tried not to spew. "Nick, listen to yourself! Your old lady? How old are you? Fifty? You're eighteen years old and you're engaged to be married? Snap out of it! Act your age. Be yourself."

"Like you?" Nick asked sarcastically.

"Hell yeah, like me," I told him. "Feel free to use me as a role model."

"You're the one who should be yourself," he said.

"What's that supposed to mean? I am myself."

"No you're not," Nick said. He took off his glasses and cleaned them with his shirt. "You're never yourself, Higgs, not even when you're alone. You're always putting on. Samantha says that you're a phony."

"What are you talking about?" I asked. "Have you gone nuts? Samantha's manipulative, bossy, and all wrong for you."

"She says the same thing about you," Nick said glumly. I'd never seen him look so sad. "I'm sorry, Higgs, but I'm with Samantha for life. With you, well, you're going off to Harvard, I'm going to USC, and who knows how often we're going to see each other once summer's over."

That's when it hit me. College. We were going to college. I was going to college. Harvard. I was going to Harvard, all the way on the other side of the country. I was going to Harvard to become a dentist. A dentist.

"Are you okay?" Nick asked.

"What? Sure. Why?"

"Because you're drinking my Dr Pepper. You hate Dr Pepper."

I put it down. "Sorry. I got distracted."

"Yeah, well I'm sorry too," he said.

I knew he meant it. Nick never lied to me.

Day 6

CHAPTER 9

When we entered the debate room after lunch, the talking stopped. However, Rosalee Gomez seemed to have no problem with her vocal cords. "Good morning, Master Debater," she said, waving a flyer in my face.

I didn't reply.

"Love your slogan," Rosalee continued. Her voice was dripping with more snark than usual. "'Higgs for Dinky Dick of the Year.' It's very catchy."

I could feel my face start to get red. At least I no longer broke out in hives like I used to when I was younger. "Are you proud of yourself, Rosalee?" I asked. "You're the one behind the flyers, admit it."

Rosalee emitted a high-pitched laugh that sounded like the French fry timer at Benny's B-Burgers. "Higgs, you're nothing but a pig — and I don't waste my time on pigs, unless they're barbecued and served with coleslaw on the side."

"You're deluding yourself, Rosalee. Not even a pig would allow you in their mud pit. You might get it dirty."

It was so obvious. Of course. Of course, it was Rosalee. Who else could it have been?

Coach Valcorza sprinted over to us. He was wearing one of his many monogrammed shirts, and today's tie was paisley. Coach was one of the only teachers at Sally Ride High who wore a tie to school. Every year, debate team members would try to outdo one another by giving him the ugliest Christmas tie we could find. Nick won last year with one that featured a photo of a mean-looking cat dressed as an elf.

"If you two are going to debate, at least do it parliamentary style," Coach Valcorza said.

Rosalee and I glared at each other, neither one of us willing to back down.

Someone in the back of the room shouted, "Smackdown!"

Another person shouted, "Go, Dinky Dick!"

"I'm game," Rosalee said, flipping her mess of black hair over her shoulder. "You man enough, Higgs?"

"I may not be as manly as you, Rosalee," I told her. "But I'm man enough to decimate you in a debate."

There was a buzz in the air as we each took our place behind a podium.

"Because we are forgoing the twenty-minute prep time, this will be an ad hoc parliamentary debate, and we'll play loose with the rules," Coach Valcorza announced cheerfully. "You can even combine your affirmatives and negatives and/or rebuttals with questioning. Do you both agree?"

We nodded.

In a way, I felt sorry for Rosalee. She was in for a rude surprise if she thought she could outdebate me. Sure, Rosalee may have been the national champion in Dramatic Interpretation, but that was a bogus win. Dramatic Interp was merely acting out someone else's words. Imagine doing a passage from *My Sister's Keeper*, over and over and over again, and thinking that there was any skill to that.

As for me? At state finals, Nick and I swept first place, again, and I took home the first-place speaker trophy to add to my collection. At nationals, we made it to semifinals, and would have gone to finals if that team from Scarsdale hadn't won on a bogus topicality technicality.

"Let's do this!" Coach Valcorza shouted, pumping his fist in the air. There was nothing he loved better than a spirited debate. "Shall we flip a coin and see who's affirmative?"

I bowed to Rosalee. "Why not let Ms. Gomez be affirmative and choose the topic?"

Chivalry was not dead, but with any luck, it would be the death of my opponent.

Rosalee's eyes widened. "Any topic?" she asked warily. Rosalee had debated a bit, but only as a floater if someone was sick. "Not one of this year's resolutions?"

"Your choice," I said generously. "Make one up. Anything you want. Anything." I was feeling generous. "Think of it as my graduation gift to you."

She stared at me, as if waiting for the punch line. None came. "All right, then," Rosalee said. She bit her pen and began scribbling furiously on her legal pad.

"Who would like to judge?" Coach Valcorza asked. Two

varsity debaters and a JV girl raised their hands. I tried not to smile. The guys were friends of mine and routinely made fun of Rosalee behind her back. She was one of those let's-castrate-all-men feminists, so most of the guys were too afraid to openly mock her, for fear that she would do them bodily harm.

I studied Rosalee and tried to second-guess her topic. The death penalty? Immigration? Medical marijuana? No problem. I had those all covered, pro and con. Plus, I'd been clocked at speaking over three hundred words per minute. The poor girl didn't stand a chance.

I took a deep breath. This was to be my last debate, ever. Even though Harvard had a stellar debate team, I had decided against joining. Just because I was an undergrad at Harvard, that didn't guarantee that I'd get into their dental school. Harvard Dental only took thirty-five students a year, and it meant that in my first four years I'd need to ace organic chemistry, microbiology, physics, biochemistry . . . the scope of my collegiate commitment to a dentistry career was beginning to dawn on me. Honestly, I had been so focused on getting in that I never thought to look beyond an acceptance letter. And the only thing that piqued my interest during the campus tour was Harvard's Community Garden — an ambitious student-run model for sustainable urban gardening.

Coach Valcorza nodded to Rosalee. "Okay," he said, "affirmative constructive — you've got six minutes . . . go."

He clicked his stopwatch.

Rosalee cleared her throat, gripped the sides of the podium, and began. "Resolved: Higgs Boson Bing is an asshole and therefore should immediately be stripped of his debate captain status —"

Day 6

CHAPTER 10

Groans and cheers echoed in the room after Rosalee stated her ridiculous proposition. Coach Valcorza rubbed what little hair he had with both hands, a habit he had when he was nervous. We used to joke that he had a full head of hair at the beginning of the school year, and was always bald at the end.

Rosalee's argument was totally out of the realm of rational debate, and she reveled in it. She stopped slouching and her voice rose as she continued her assault. Rosalee Gomez was on fire and she knew it.

"One: Higgs Boson Bing is known as a powerhouse debater. However," she continued, "it is common knowledge that his partner, Nicholas 'Nick' Milgram, does the majority of the research, writing, and prep, rendering Higgs little more than a talking head.

"Two: While Higgs Boson Bing is well *known* on campus, that does not equate to well *liked*, and therefore this reflects poorly on the debate team. His popularity was mostly due to his relationship with Rosemary 'Roo' Wynn, plus the awards heaped upon him by faculty who he has conned into thinking he is a somebody.

"Three: Higgs Boson Bing twists the truth to get what he wants. He is unethical, unprincipled, and equivocates to such a degree that false statements should be renamed Bing-isms."

As Rosalee rambled on with her slander, I looked around the room. Some of the girls were cheering. A lot of the varsity guys were laughing. Coach Valcorza looked amused, though I was not. Clearly, Rosalee was out of control and her arguments had no substance — like her. I thought back to the night we shared at Howard Johnson's and realized that she was hell-bent on exacting her revenge.

A third of the class, who happened to all be female, broke out in wild applause when Rosalee was done. I was momentarily speechless. I glanced at Nick, who looked as shocked as I was.

Okay, okay. Two can play at this game, I thought.

I took a deep breath and consulted my notes. Coach Valcorza gave me six minutes for my opposition speech, coupled with a cross-exam, and I was determined to make the most of it.

"My esteemed, or shall I say 'steamed,' opponent is confused," I began slowly before ramping up my assault. "Ms. Gomez throws out so many false premises that it is a wonder her arguments don't implode. She is so vague that I can barely see her. This much is true: Higgs Boson Bing is a 'somebody,' as confirmed by his acceptance into Harvard University. As to Ms. Gomez's contentions, they are weak prima facie arguments that are nothing less than fabrications of a — how can I put this nicely? Of a . . . deranged mind.

46

"The debate duo of Higgs Boson Bing and Nicolas 'Nick' Milgram, California State Champions two years in a row, is indeed a team. What evidence," I said forcefully, "do you have that Milgram carried Bing, and not the other way around?"

Rosalee stood ramrod straight and stared at the back wall. "Mr. Milgram's girlfriend, Samantha Verve, told me," she said.

I was taken aback, but quickly gained my composure. "Can you elaborate?"

"Ms. Verve said that Nick said that he was getting tired of doing all the work and Higgs getting all the glory."

I waved my hand dismissively. "Hearsay," I informed the judges with a smirk. I looked at Nick, but he was playing with his cell phone. "You contend that Higgs Boson Bing is popular, but not well liked," I continued. "Can you quantify this?"

"Well, I don't have actual numbers, but —"

"Can you quantify this?" I asked, loudly. Always speak to the back of the room, Coach Valcorza had taught us.

"McDonald's hamburgers are the most popular, but it doesn't make them any good," she said by way of evidence. "As for Higgs, everyone says that he's a jerk, but they don't want to cross him because —"

"Ms. Gomez," I said, cutting her off. "Need I remind you that we are not discussing hamburgers, but rather, someone's reputation? You ought to know that plucking rumors out of the clouds is not solid evidence. Your second point has no merit. As for your third accusation, that Mr. Bing is unethical, unprincipled, and . . ." I checked my notes. ". . . equivocates," I continued, "it is fiction. Where is the proof for this?"

"Yes," Rosalee answered. "I would be happy to. You — er, Mr.

Bing created a bogus social service organization called the Society of Animal Protection, a.k.a. SAP. You then included it on your Harvard application —"

"Ms. Gomez," I shouted. "Again, hearsay. You have no proof, no evidence, that what you are contending is true. Furthermore, yours is merely a slanderous case of rumored misconduct, clearly delivered because you have some sort of ongoing grudge against the aforementioned Mr. Bing. Your insinuations are pathetic, really. . . ."

I couldn't let her know that I was rattled. Did Nick really say that to Samantha? Did some people actually dislike me? What did Rosalee know about SAP and my Harvard application?

"Ms. Gomez," Coach Valcorza said. "Seven minutes for the affirmative."

I cracked my knuckles. I was always able to poke holes in my opponent's arguments. That was where I shined. Normally, I was energized at this point in a debate. However, when I looked over at Rosalee, she winked at me and then blew me a kiss, and for the first time I doubted myself.

Day 6

CHAPTER 11

Whoa, Nick, wait up!"

He was hurrying out of the debate room. "Can't talk to you, remember."

"Right," I replied. "Because of my moral compass. Hey, did you really say that stuff to Samantha?"

"I don't remember," he said, keeping his head down. "Look, I gotta go."

I watched him disappear into the crowd. It was only when Zander Findley coughed into his hand and said, "Dinky Dick," that I remembered the flyers. I felt like I had been hit with a solid one-two punch. Where was Mr. French? Mr. Avis promised that the janitor would be getting rid of them.

As I ripped down the flyers, Zander followed closely behind asking in his obnoxious pseudo-intellectual voice, "How does it feel to know you are despised?

"Why did you refuse to save Roo's life?

"How dinky is your dick, Higgs?

"Did you really cheat on your Harvard application?"

Had that rumor already ignited? I wondered. I pivoted and started to light into him — "Zan . . . Zan . . . Zan . . ." To my horror, I couldn't get his name out. Panic struck. My throat constricted. I shook my head and tried to ignore Zander, who was looking more smug than usual in his stupid brown corduroy jacket, despite the 85-degree heat.

As I pushed through the crowd, I ripped down more flyers along the way — and the more I tore down, the more pissed I became. I spotted Mr. French laughing and talking on his cell phone.

"Excuse me," I said. "But aren't *you* supposed to be taking these down?"

Mr. French looked at me like I was garbage. "Do I work for you?" he asked, putting his phone away. When he smiled, his crooked teeth showed. My teeth are perfect, thanks to my father, "the painless dentist," and his colleague, Dr. Caprio, "the straight-up orthodontist."

"Technically, yes you do," I told him. "My parents pay taxes. Mr. Avis assured me that the flyers would be disposed of."

"Did he, now?" Mr. French drawled. Despite his name, he spoke with a Southern accent. Rumor had it that he was a Sally Ride High School star quarterback twenty years ago and had earned a football scholarship, but his grades rendered him ineligible. "Well," Mr. French said, "I'll be sure to get right on it."

"Thank you," I said, turning around to leave.

"Yeah," he continued, raising his voice. "It will be my pleasure to take down the flyers, since I have nothing better to do and you, college boy, are so important. Oh, and by the way, this is called a trash can," he explained, motioning to one. "These are for trash."

Clearly, Mr. French must have sustained head injuries during his football days.

"Do you know what a trash can looks like?" he asked, as if speaking to a toddler.

"Yes?" I said. I didn't know what kind of game he was playing.

"Good," Mr. French said.

"I gotta go," I said awkwardly. He was starting to creep me out.

As I raced down the empty hall, I could hear him laughing.

In AP Literature, Ms. Gill was telling us about the time she saw her favorite author, Sherman Alexie, at the airport but was too starstruck to say anything. As she recounted how she followed him to baggage claim, I looked around the room. I was no longer convinced it had to be Rosalee Gomez who put up the flyers. For all I knew, it could have been Mr. Avis, or even Mr. French, or most likely Zander Findley.

I started a list.

I divided the yellow legal pad into two columns. The first one was for people who might hold a grudge against me. The second ranked their capacity for revenge on a 1 to 10 scale, with 10 being "Death to Higgs." At first, I decided just to include people from the last year of high school. Then I changed my mind and listed everyone from anytime. Who knew about these psychopaths? They could have been harboring a grudge for years.

By the time the bell rang, I was shocked. I had used up two pages, and I wasn't done yet.

Day 6

CHAPTER 12

"Hey, honey," Mom said when I got home. She was still wrapped in her Robe of Depression. "I thought you'd be staying after school since this is your last week."

Charlie was sitting at the kitchen counter, eating a scone. She began to laugh when she saw me.

"What's so funny?" my mother asked. She looked down at the spatula in her hand as if surprised to see it.

"Higgs got a lot of publicity today," Charlie said with faux innocence.

Mom handed the spatula to Charlie and gave me a hug. "Why, that's wonderful, Higgs. You want to tell me about it?"

"Yes, Higgs," Charlie said. "Tell Mom all about it."

"Go to hell, Charles," I said.

As I marched down the hall, I could hear my mother yell, "Higgs! Come back right now and apologize to your sister!"

I flopped onto my bed. The navy-blue quilt had the Harvard crest on it, alongside the crest of the Harvard dental school.

Grammy Bing had made it for Jeffrey to take to college. After he died, my parents gave it to me. I inherited most of his things, like his board games, and his police memorabilia, and his Rubik's Cube collection.

Jeffrey could solve a Rubik's Cube faster than anyone I knew. It took him over a year, but he taught me how to solve them too. Then there was the Los Angeles Police Department stuff, like the badge he got on eBay, and the California penal code book his best friend, Connor Douglas, had given him. They'd play this game where one of them would make up a crime, and the other would tell them how many laws they broke.

We used to have Sunday Family Game Night. But without Jeffrey to organize them, they just stopped. I once asked why we didn't have them anymore, and my father said, "Game Night would have stopped anyway once Jeffrey went off to Harvard." I guess it had never occurred to any of us to continue it without him.

My bookshelves were packed. Half with books, the other half with Kram Notes. Both were in alphabetical order. On my desk was a neat pile of college acceptance letters. The one from Harvard was on top. Dad wanted to get that one framed and hang it next to Jeffrey's acceptance letter in his den — which was next to my father's Harvard letter, and my grandfather's. A legacy of Bings.

I picked up a photo of Roo and me in front of the Sleeping Beauty Castle at Disneyland. We were both wearing Mickey Mouse ears and looked deliriously happy. I guess we were then, and for a moment, I missed her. The trouble was that out of our over two years together, we had maybe four good months total.

There was a knock on the door.

"Higgs, we need to talk."

Mom looked worried.

"Sure. What?"

"Charlie told me what happened at school."

I could feel my body tense.

"Is it true?" she asked. "Were there disparaging flyers of you all around campus?"

"Did Charlie tell you what they said?"

Mom shook her head. "She said to ask you."

My sister strolled past my room and waved as if she were on a Rose Parade float.

"Nothing to worry about, Mom," I assured her. "It was just a little prank, but I've got it under control."

"You're sure?" my mother said. She pushed her hands into the deep pockets of her bathrobe. For the first time, I noticed how much she had aged. She had stopped dying her hair, and the gray had suddenly outnumbered the brown.

"Are you okay?" I asked.

"Higgs, honey" — her voice cracked — "I'm going to miss you so much."

"You'll still have Dad and Charlie," I reminded her.

"That's not the same as having you here," she said.

"I can hear you!" Charlie yelled from her room. She was always hanging around the edges, eavesdropping.

After Mom left, I shut the door and retrieved a crumpled flyer from my backpack. I set it next to my list of suspects. I called Nick, but before he answered, I hung up. I considered calling Roo, but decided that was a bad idea. Who could I call?

Who could I trust? Who could I talk to? I drew a complete blank.

I flashed back to Rosalee's argument: "While Higgs Boson Bing is well *known* on campus, that does not equate to well *liked*, and therefore this reflects poorly on the debate team. His popularity was mostly due to his relationship with Rosemary 'Roo' Wynn. . . ."

What if what she said was true? I used to be proud of the fact that everyone knew me. But to follow Rosalee's logic, everyone knew who Hitler was, and he certainly wasn't well liked. I headed out to my garden to clear my head. It was the only place I felt at peace. Who would take care of it when I was gone? Dad was too busy. Mom was too preoccupied. Charlie was too obstinate.

When I was a freshman, I was in a constant state of anxiety. Middle school had been a breeze compared to high school. High school mattered. If I was going to get into Harvard, I couldn't afford to be anything less than perfect. After the first few months of class, everyone sorted themselves out. My crowd was the student government, Advanced Placement, do-everything-or-die college group.

Later, many of us had the same college coach, took the same SAT prep classes, and toured the same universities. We agonized over the AP exams together, wrote and rewrote our college essays, and bonded over the Common Application. We encouraged one another, even though we didn't mean it. Anyone applying to the same school was competition. Everyone was scheming to get an edge on the next person. The pressure was intense and stretching the truth was not only a given, it was expected. Our school counselors said as much.

"Do whatever it takes," they'd say, leaving us to sort out the implication.

For Sally Ride High School Helps Week, all the seniors were required to do community service. I created the Society for Animal Protection as a joke. Everyone loves animals. So what if SAP only had two members, me and Nick? We protected an animal.

I wrote a script that was full of drama and pathos. Then we took Captain Kirk and rolled him in the mud. That would be Nick's Goldendoodle, Captain Kirk; not the man, Captain Kirk. We made a video about how we rescued this poor animal. Nick and I got an A on the project and the video was even shown at assembly. At the last minute, I included it on my Harvard application.

I applied to twelve colleges: Princeton, Harvard, Brown, USC, NYU, Yale, Oxford, Cambridge, Columbia, UC Berkeley, Caltech, and UC Davis. Davis was my safety school. I got into every place but Oxford and Caltech. However, once I received my early admission to Harvard, none of the others mattered. I didn't even bother responding to their letters.

The tomatoes were growing in red and ripe. They'd be ready to pick in a couple of days. I gathered some zucchini for Mom, and a head of cauliflower. The artichokes looked good. I threw some of those in the basket for old Mrs. Yaseen from down the street. Once a week, since I was ten, I'd bring her fruits and vegetables. I stopped to admire my Bing cherries. They were, of course, perfect. All the neighbors said that my produce was better than the stuff they got in the store.

When I was younger and couldn't sleep, I'd sneak outside and just sit in the middle of the plants, listening to the crickets, looking at the stars. My mother must have known about this. How could she not? There was always dirt in my bed in the morning. But she never mentioned it then, or now. Neither did I.

This time even the garden couldn't calm me down. After I brought everything inside, I was still feeling antsy, like there was a pressure building up inside of me. I had to do something, or I'd explode.

I laced up my running shoes.

Day 6

CHAPTER 13

The billboard read "Brookhaven Villas — Where CommUnity Matters."

The developers had been lobbying hard to get the subdivision built, but it had languished for years. Brookhaven abutted an industrial park fronted by a run-down strip mall, and was about half a mile from my house. Still, it seemed like another country. It was heavily wooded and the terrain was hilly. At the very peak stood the old, abandoned water tower.

I ran under the billboard and onto the dirt path where Jeffrey used to take me exploring. I checked my watch. My time was good. Better than good. Had the entire school turned on me? A couple of flyers would have been funny. I had a sense of humor. But dozens? And "Dinky Dick"? How cold was that? The stress gave me enough fuel to run full out. I ran until my lungs burned and would have kept going if not for the sudden cramp in my left leg. I was a high jumper, not a runner. I slowed and tried to walk off the pain.

Down by the dry riverbank were old car carcasses, broken chairs, a wooden doghouse without a roof. I wandered among the discards of other people's lives, wishing I could toss aside my last twenty-four hours and start over. When I got to the gravel pit, I stopped. Jeffrey and I had never wandered past that. I don't know anyone who had.

Everyone had heard the rumors — brutal murders had occurred in the woods, and that's where the bodies were buried. Or that it wasn't a gravel pit at all, but quicksand, and that an entire family, including grandparents and a dog, died there. Jeffrey was the bravest person I knew, but even he'd say, "We'd better be safe and go home." I never asked him what he thought was on the other side.

By now, the gravel pit wasn't much of anything anymore. Loose rocks in a shallow hole in the ground less than half a block's length. It didn't look nearly as imposing as it did nine years ago.

My first steps were tentative, and the ground was unsteady. But the more I walked, the firmer the footing. On the other side, I was met with an endless thicket of plants. My better judgment told me to give up. To go home. Yet I kept moving forward. I swatted away the overgrown brush until I came to a clearing.

In the distance, tucked behind some trees, I could make out something big and gray. It was an old Airstream trailer. I picked up a handful of rocks and threw them at the relic. They made a satisfying thud. I bet myself that I could hit the door of the trailer five times in a row. I did that sometimes. Made bets with myself. Like, when I was driving, if I could make all the green lights, it meant that I'd get an acceptance letter in the mail. Or, if I could get seven girls in a row to say hi to me, it meant that I'd ace a test. Or, if I could throw ten paper wads into the trash can across my room, I wouldn't feel depressed.

One, two, three . . . I was nailing the target every time. When I started thinking about the flyers, I threw harder. Four, FIVE . . . I could have kept on going forever. Then, out of nowhere, someone yelled, "STOP IT!!!!"

I froze.

"Are you done?" an angry voice said.

It was coming from inside the Airstream.

"Well, are you?" the voice asked.

"Uh, yeah. Sure. I guess," I answered.

The door opened and a girl about my age emerged.

"What exactly were you trying to do, dumbass?" she said, scowling.

Even though I was shaken, I found myself walking toward her.

She had short black hair and she was wearing a flowing black dress. On her feet were old-fashioned black button-up boots, the kind Mary Poppins might have worn. Her eyes were rimmed with black too. The only color on her pale face was her bright red lips. She looked scary, like she had escaped from a Wonton Weasels music video.

"I'm s-sorry," I stammered. "I didn't know anyone was inside. Do you . . . do you live in there?"

I'd heard rumors that a few homeless people lived in Brookhaven and would have to be relocated if the development took place.

The girl looked conflicted. "Yeah," she finally said. "Yeah, I live here. So what? I would invite you in, but I don't want to."

I couldn't tell if she was serious or mocking me.

I extended my hand. "Hello, I'm Higgs Boson Bing."

When she didn't take it, I ran my hand through my hair as if I had intended to do that all along.

"I'm Hadron Collider," she said with a smirk.

"What?" I asked. It felt as if the rotation of the earth had suddenly shifted.

"Hadron Collider," she said again. Her hazel-blue eyes bored through mine and made me squirm. "Surely, you've heard of me. I'm the world's largest and highest energy particle accelerator. I was used to discover the elusive Higgs boson, the God particle, and I guess I've found him, right here, trying to destroy my home."

I laughed, aware that it sounded fake. Okay, so she was toying with me. I was impressed that she knew about the Higgs boson and the Hadron Collider. On the day the massive energy particle accelerator identified the elusive Higgs boson, my mother wept — only this time they were tears of joy. "Do you know what this means for science?" she said.

"It means another reason my brother, Higgs Boson, will get a lot of attention," my sister said, not even trying to hide the disgust in her voice.

"Most people don't even know what Higgs boson is," I told the girl.

"I'm not most people," she said.

"What's your name?" There was a butterfly tattoo on her arm. When she caught me staring, I felt my face flush.

"Monarch," she finally said. "You can call me Monarch."

"Okay, Monarch," I said. "It's nice to meet you."

"Isn't it, though," Monarch said without a trace of affectation. "You got a cigarette?"

I shook my head. "No."

"Damn," she said. "I could really use a smoke."

"Smoking will stain your teeth," I told her.

"What are you, a dentist?" she asked.

"Not yet," I answered.

Monarch was nothing like the girls at Sally Ride High School. If Roo or Samantha ever came across her, they'd probably hand over their purses and run away screaming. Monarch had an edge to her, like you would expect from someone who lived on the streets. Warning signs were going off in my head. Every part of me was saying that this person was bad news.

I opened my mouth and heard myself say, "I could go get you a pack of cigarettes."

"Would you, Higgs Boson?" she said, fluttering her eyelashes at me. I thought she was being sarcastic, but couldn't be sure. I felt off balance, but in a good way.

"Uh, sure. Is there anything else you want? A candy bar or something? Chips?"

She gave this some serious thought before stating, "A Butterfinger. Yeah, cigs and a Butterfinger. That sounds about right."

"Be right back," I told her. "Don't go anywhere."

I took off running, forgetting that I had a leg cramp.

Day 6

CHAPTER 14

The shabby strip mall near the entrance to Brookhaven hosted a Supremo Dry Cleaners, Mixxed Martial Arts A Academy, and a Jiffy Mart, only the "J" was missing so the sign read "iffy Mart." The only car in the parking lot was a silver BMW with a "Trust me, I'm a lawyer" bumper sticker.

I had sprinted all the way there, and was still out of breath as I scanned the candy aisle searching for a Butterfinger. It was then that I realized that I didn't have any money.

"Can I get this and some cigarettes and pay you back later?" I asked the guy behind the counter.

"Can I be the king of England?" he asked.

"I guess that means no?"

"How did you get to be so smart?"

That Monarch was waiting for me was all I could think about as I ran home. Talking to her got my adrenaline soaring, but in a good way, like when Nick and I went to nationals for debate. My leg was killing me, but the rest of me was just fine.

I took the front porch stairs two at a time, grabbed my wallet and car keys, and was almost out the door, when I heard, "Higgs! A moment of your time, please."

Shit. What was Dad doing home early? Usually, he was late. Sometimes he didn't come home at all.

Reluctantly, I entered his den and stood behind the leather chair opposite his massive desk. Dad's office was a shrine to Harvard.

"Your sister told me what happened at school today." He was still wearing his white lab coat with "Dr. Charles A. Bing, DDS" embroidered above the pocket. When I got into Harvard, his gift to me was a matching lab coat with "Dr. Higgs B. Bing, DDS" on it. "I know you're not at Harvard Dental yet, but you're on your way!" he had exclaimed.

"So, who's out to get you?" Dad asked.

"No one. It's no big deal," I said, looking at the clock. I could have killed Charlie right then, only that would have delayed me even longer. Monarch was waiting for me.

"Defamation of character is a big deal," he said. "Remember when Trent Tenafly called me a fraud?"

I nodded. We all remembered that.

"Someone has it out for you, Higgs," Dad continued. He refilled his Scotch glass. "It's a Trent Tenafly situation, and we can't just ignore this."

Trent Tenafly was his sworn enemy. A rival dentist whose slogan was "the pain-free dentist," as opposed to my father's "painless dentist." Both claim the other copied them. They've been enemies for so long, neither can recall who started it.

I looked at the clock again and started to fidget.

"I've got it under control," I assured him. "Um, Dad, there's somewhere I need to be right now."

"What's more important than talking to your old man?" he asked, offering me a grin. His perfect teeth were his own best advertising.

"Nothing. Nothing is," I said. "But I've really got to be somewhere."

He got up, winked, and slapped me on the back. "Okay, son. You go where you need to be, and tell Roo I said hi."

I didn't correct him.

Like everyone else, my parents loved Roo. If I told my father that I was buying cigarettes for a tattooed stranger, he wouldn't have let me off so easily.

By the time I drove back to Brookhaven, the sun was setting. I pulled into the empty iffy Mart parking lot, made my purchases, and scrambled across the gravel pit. I didn't slow until I neared the Airstream trailer. "Monarch?" I called out.

There was no answer.

"Monarch," I said again, this time louder. "It's me, Higgs. Higgs Bing. Higgs Boson Bing."

When no one responded, I rapped politely on the door.

Nothing.

"Are you in there?" I slowly opened the door, half scared of what I might find.

It wasn't what I was expecting.

Instead of a mosh pit of garbage, the Airstream was surprisingly clean. Sparse, but clean, as if Monarch had taken pains to make it into a home. There were a couple of Paris subway maps on the wall, and on the counter were a tin of cookies, a jar of peanut butter, a chipped white plate, and utensils. A battered beach chair sat next to a small table made from a couple of old suitcases that could probably pass as vintage on eBay. In the corner were a little pillow and a thin blue blanket like the ones from an airplane. A Coleman lantern sat on the floor next to a small stack of books. Jack Kerouac, Albert Camus, Victor Hugo.

I left the cigarettes and Butterfinger on the table.

Tuesday

Day 5

CHAPTER 15

All night, my thoughts had ricocheted from Roo to Monarch to Rosalee to Monarch to Dinky Dick to Monarch. Suffice to say, I didn't get any sleep, which was actually typical during my high school years. Sleep was something that had eluded me. My mother never slept either. While I'd be up studying, she would roam around the house in her Robe of Depression, talking to Jeffrey's portrait, or waiting up for my father, who was unapologetic about his many city council, Rotary, and dental association meetings, fund-raisers, and mixers.

"I can't let these people down" was his typical excuse. "They need me."

Charlie stood impatiently by the back door. Her cello case looked like an upright body bag. "Let's GO!" she shouted.

"There are only three days left of school," I reminded her. "We can be late for once."

"Four days," she said sullenly. "Only seniors get Friday off."

I was in no hurry to get to school. If anything, for the first time in my life, I was dreading it. If one more person called me Dinky Dick, I thought I might lose it. For the record, I might not be in the porn star category, but still, there was nothing dinky about me.

"Let's go!" Charlie yelled, again.

"In a minute," I yelled back. I was in the backyard picking apples for Mrs. Sanchez. The only thing she loved more than my apples were my peaches, but those weren't quite ripe yet.

The drive to school was typical. I'd have KJAZ on and Charlie would change to KiND, the indie alternative experimental station that was so underground it sounded like they were broadcasting from the center of the earth. We'd fight and, neither of us willing to concede, would end up listening to something like REO Speedwagon's "Can't Fight This Feeling," or some other 1980s throwback song that we both despised.

At school, the old green Kia with the broken window had claimed my parking lot space, so I was forced to park Rolvo in the street again. Rolvo was what Charlie and I had nicknamed the car.

Red + Volvo = Rolvo

Before I had turned off the engine, Charlie jumped out. "See you later," she said, tossing a half-eaten apple at me.

As my sister hauled her cello toward school, I hung back finishing the rest of the apple. Who was out to get me? I wondered. And why? What kind of asshole would target me like that?

The closer I got to the rusted Kia the more pissed I became. Without giving it a second thought, I tossed the apple core through the open window. Before it even landed, I regretted my move. I was about to reach in and retrieve it when someone said, "Hey, Higgs?"

Startled, I looked up. It was Nick — and there was no Samantha with him. I grinned. It was about time we talked. I hoped we'd have a good laugh over Samantha's "moral compass" statement, plus I couldn't wait to tell him about Monarch.

"Nicholas!" I cried, slapping him on the back.

Nick looked miserable. "Just checking to see how you are doing," he said. "And to warn you."

"Warn me about what?"

"Word around campus is that whoever did the flyers isn't done with you yet."

I could feel my face heat up. "What have you heard?"

Nick shook his head. "Seriously, that's all I know. It's just a rumor, but watch your back. Look, I gotta go. I can't be seen talking to you."

"You're joking, right?" I said. "Nick, we've been best friends forever."

He looked like he was on the verge of tears. "I know," he said. "But I'm getting married to Samantha, not you."

Even when we were young, Nick and I looked out for each other. Last year, when Coach Valcorza named me speech and debate captain, he said I could pick my co-captain. Everyone was certain that I'd pick Rosalee Gomez, because (1) co-captains have always been a guy and girl, and (2) Rosalee won nationals twice in Dramatic Interpretation, and (3) Coach strongly suggested I pick Rosalee.

So when I said, "This year's co-captain will be ... Nick Milgram," everyone was shocked, especially Nick.

"I'm not sure if this is right," he whispered to me as all the guys in the room applauded.

"You can thank me later," I answered.

After that, Rosalee stopped talking to me, which was actually a good thing. Coach Valcorza took me aside and said, "I know that I said that the final decision would be up to you, but are you sure you want Nick and not Rosalee?"

I told him that my choice was final. But what I couldn't say was that it would have been impossible to co-captain with Rosalee. Sure, she was an excellent public speaker, but she was an awful kisser.

The team was in San Diego at state finals our sophomore year, and Rosalee and I were both celebrating wins: she for taking first place with her dramatic interpretation of *The House of Blue Leaves*, and I for being named First Speaker, Varsity Division, Debate. Everyone had gone to their hotel rooms, leaving me and Rosalee in a dark corner of the damp Howard Johnson's lobby. As ESPN blared on the television, Rosalee leaned in and kissed me. I wasn't sure what to do, so, as not to be rude, I kissed her back.

Big mistake.

It was like making out with a Nerf ball. Her lips were spongy and kissing her was entirely without passion. I felt nothing — well, maybe total awkwardness, and I couldn't wait to get away. Then there was that issue of Roo. We had just started going out, and though we weren't official, it seemed highly likely that it could happen, especially since Roo had been dropping heavy hints like, "Gee Higgs, I bet you'd make a great boyfriend."

It goes unsaid that when the debate team travels, we don't narc on each other. Many hookups and heartbreaks have gone on during speech and debate tournaments. Last year, an extemporaneous speaker from Salt Lake City made it very clear to Nick that she was willing to sleep with him. All he had to do was say "affirmative," and the deal would have been done.

I told Nick that whatever he decided, I'd keep it from Roo, and therefore, Samantha. In the end, he declined and Miss Salt Lake City found a debater from Des Moines who was more than willing to accept her offer. The downside was that Nick felt so guilty that he confessed what happened (or didn't happen) to Samantha, including my comment. She had hated me ever since.

Anyway, the next morning after our quasi kissing, Rosalee made it a point to sit next to me on the team bus, even going so far as asking Nick to move. She was the last person I wanted to see. Not that she was ugly. But let's face it — she was no Roo.

As the bus pulled into the school parking lot, I told Rosalee that even though she was really nice, what happened at the Howard Johnson's was a one-time deal, never to be spoken of again. Then I added, "I have a girlfriend."

"You never told me you were with someone," Rosalee said, eyes flashing, lips pursed into a hard line.

At that point, I hadn't even told Roo.

"Yes!" Roo squealed when I asked her to be my girlfriend. "Tell me, Higgs, why do you think we belong together?"

I made up something mushy and that seemed to satisfy her. What I couldn't tell Roo was that we were together so I wouldn't have to kiss Rosalee again.

I wondered what it would be like to kiss Monarch. Would she pull away? Would she lean into it? I liked to imagine that kissing her would start off slow, teasing, lips barely brushing against each other, then quickly build into an all-consuming intensity that would leave both of us breathless. Kissing Roo was nice, especially in the beginning. But there were never any fireworks. It was more like sparklers.

When Roo and I first got together, I gave us six months, tops. After six months, I gave us another three months, and then another three months, then another, until suddenly two years, four months, and seven days had passed. During the last year, I was determined to break up with Roo, but had never gotten around to it. What I could not have imagined was that breaking up with Roo would mean that I was breaking up with Nick too.

Day 5

CHAPTER 16

Most of the offending flyers were gone, except for a few strays that I tore down. However, that didn't stop people from mocking me. It was as if everyone had suddenly been given permission to let loose. Guys, who one week earlier would have stepped aside when I walked down the hall, were now calling me Dinky Dick, or just Dinky, but we all knew what they meant. Most of the girls glared at me, but I think that was more because of the kidney hypothetical than the flyers. You know how when people break up, their friends take sides? Well, it felt like the entire school took Roo's side.

When I entered the band room, the drum section heated up and then the horns jumped in, as wind instruments shouted, "Dinky Dick!" Soon the whole room was playing Elvis Costello's "Pump It Up."

I had to laugh, because crying was never an option. "Hey, fellow dickheads," I shouted. "You all suck!"

I glanced at Charlie, who was sawing away on her cello. She

was playing "Pomp and Circumstance" and had succeeded in making it sound like a funeral dirge. When she didn't meet my gaze, I wondered if I was an embarrassment to her.

"Thettle down, thettle down," Mr. Hermes, the band director, yelled. He was used to our antics, having been in a real band once. When he was younger, he toured with the Muskrats & Sara Sue for two years. You could sort of tell that he had a life apart from SRHS. Despite his grayish hair, which was worn long and often in a ponytail, Mr. Hermes had an air of perpetual youth. His T-shirts featured bands no one had ever heard of and he was a human catalogue of rock music. I liked Mr. Hermes. Even though I had to miss a lot of jazz band events because of debate, he never marked me down for it. In return, unlike some of the others, I never once made fun of his lisp. I would never joke about a speech impediment. Never.

Even though most of the kids stopped playing Elvis Costello when Mr. Hermes ordered them to, Zander Findley kept going. He never knew when to stop.

As Mr. Hermes rehearsed the band for graduation, the seniors sat out since we'd be picking up our diplomas. I looked at my list of suspects. I had narrowed the list down to eleven. There were now eleven total. Eleven people who would have loved to see me fall on my face.

United States criminal law summarizes that a jury needs the following to be convinced of a person's guilt . . .

1. Means
2. Motive
3. Opportunity

Based on that, I instantly ruled out five names, leaving the following suspects:

Rosalee Gomez
Mr. Avis
Mr. French
Zander Findley
Roo and/or Samantha

And finally,

Nick

Day 5

CHAPTER 17

"They're here!"

Reflections/snoitcelfeR had arrived. That was the name of our yearbook which, as far as I could figure, had nothing to do with our school name, Sally Ride High School. One, two, three . . . seven, eight . . . twelve, thirteen. I was on thirteen pages. I scanned the index. There was only one person on more pages than me, Zander Findley; however, that was to be expected since he was co-editor of the yearbook. Rosalee Gomez was on as many pages as I was, but only because she joined every dork club imaginable, like the Junior Philatelic Society and the Oui, French Club. At our school, clubs were encouraged to the point of absurdity. Everyone joined as many as possible to beef up their college applications. There was the I Love Toast Club, and the Quidditch Qlub, and the Ban Bad Words Club. Roo was a founding member of the BBWC.

As I skimmed through *Reflections/snoitcelfeR*, I paused at the faculty section. Ms. Gill, my AP Lit teacher, had her arm outstretched and was holding an open book and gazing at it. In Coach Valcorza's photo, he was in the debate room raising a megaphone to his mouth. Mr. Hermes was standing on a ladder waving his baton.

The four "Four Fun" pages featured a spread devoted to "Cutest Couples." Nick and Samantha re-created the famous John Lennon/Yoko Ono *Rolling Stone* cover shot where Yoko is lying down, and John has his leg wrapped around her — except that Nick was fully clothed. Ironically, the photo of Vanessa and Janey standing side by side and not even touching almost got cut. Mr. Avis protested, saying they were lesbians and it was an inaccurate depiction of SRHS. But when Vanessa's father threatened a lawsuit, he backed down. Then there was a photo of me with Roo on my shoulders. We looked like we owned the world.

I glanced up from the yearbook and thought I saw Roo watching me from near the vending machines. But when I looked again, she wasn't there.

Rosalee made her usual pig noises when I entered the debate room. She was sitting in the back with the rest of the varsity girls. "Rematch!" one of them yelled.

I ignored her.

I had won Monday's pseudo-parliamentary debate, 2–1. My friends voted for me, Rosalee's friend voted for her. Still, partials of her arguments played over and over in my head.

1. Nick Milgram does the majority of the research, writing, and prep, rendering Higgs little more than a talking head.

2. Higgs Boson Bing is well known on campus . . . that does not equate to well liked.
3. Higgs Boson Bing . . . is unethical, unprincipled and equivocates.

Where was Nick? I wondered. There were a couple of things I needed to clear up with him.

I took out my phone and began typing.

Higgs: I know u can't talk to me, but can u text?

Nick: Not sure

Higgs: Do u really think that u did all the work?

Nick: Somewhat

Higgs: We were a team.

Nick: We were a team during the debate. I did all the research

Higgs: Not all.

Nick: Most

Higgs: If it bothered u, why didn't u say something?

Nick: I did

Higgs: I never heard it.

Nick: Exactly

Higgs: Can we just talk?

Nick: Samantha will leave me if I talk to you

Higgs: One question

Nick: What?

Higgs: Did you put up the flyers?

Nick: Shit

Higgs: Did you?

I was startled to find Nick standing next to me. When did he get there? I wondered.

"You really are a Dinky Dick if you think I'd do that to you," Nick said. He looked wounded. "Clearly, you don't think much of me. Maybe you never did. We're over, Higgs. Have a good life."

Nick retreated to the corner of the room and slumped in a chair. His head was bent down and he was texting like mad. He'd taken off his glasses and kept rubbing his eyes. I headed over to him.

Before I got halfway across the room, Rosalee stopped me. "He's right, you know. You're a shit. If anyone would know, it would be Nick, since he researches everything. *Everything*." She wasn't done with me yet. "Shame about SAP. Oh, I mean the Society of Animal Protection. You'd think a group like that would have rescued more than one pampered pet."

"Drop it, Rosalee," I said. Nick still had his head down. "This is because of Howard Johnson's, isn't it?"

Her eyes narrowed. "Don't flatter yourself, Bing. Not every girl is after you. Your inflated ego makes it hard for anyone to get near you long enough to tell you the facts, so you operate on false assumptions. It would be a shame if the world knew who you really were."

"Did you do it?" I asked flatly.

"Do what?"

"Don't act dumb."

"I never act dumb," she spit back, "which is why a girl like me is too good for you. And if you are referring to the flyers, no, it wasn't me, but I wish I had thought of it. It's about time someone knocked you off your perch."

There was a cackle over the PA system. Everyone was still. Principal Kostantino's voice came on. "Attention Sally Ride Astronauts, I am pleased to announce that Senior of the Year has been selected." I took a deep breath. "Three committees met in secret, and after much debate, we have come to a decision."

The room went quiet as everyone glanced at me. I pretended not to see them. Okay. Okay, I told myself. This was it. The culmination of my four years at Sally Ride High School. Win this and prove superior to Zander Findley. Win this and be undisputed king of Sally Ride High. Win this and honor my brother, and make Dad happy.

"The honor of Sally Ride High School's most coveted award, Senior of the Year, goes to . . ."

Day 5

CHAPTER 18

I was stunned. Lauren Fujiyama? They gave Senior of the Year to Lauren Fujiyama? Really? Lauren Fujiyama? She didn't even do a sport. Senior of the Year was supposed to be well rounded: academics, activities, *sports*. I felt like I had the wind knocked out of me. Nick looked as surprised as I was.

Lauren Fujiyama?

There was crackling again over the PA system. Maybe Principal Kostantino was going to say there had been a mistake, and that I was the real winner. Or maybe, for the first time, there were Co-Senior(s) of the Year. My brain was having trouble processing what I had just heard.

Lauren Fujiyama?

Suddenly, I tuned into the strains of the Wanton Weasels playing their hit song "Gotcha, Gotcha, by Goodness, I Gotcha." That was odd. The song stopped and a digitized voice came on. "We interrupt our musical interlude to bring you a special announcement. . . . Extensive studies have revealed that Higgs Boson Bing is a Dinky Dick . . ."

What???!!!

". . . and now, back to the Wanton Weasels."

As the music blasted, everyone in the debate room howled. Even my so-called friends.

"Dinky Dick!" someone yelled. "Oh man, Higgs. You really pissed off someone good."

I grabbed my backpack and headed to the door. Coach Valcorza stopped me. "Where are you going, Higgs?"

"I have a headache," I told him. It was true. Ever since I was little, I'd get migraines when I got really stressed, which meant that I got a lot of migraines. What I didn't tell Coach Valcorza was that I couldn't be there right now. Not without the Senior of the Year award. Not with everyone laughing at me.

"I'll give you a pass for the nurse's office," he said.

I took my time even though my headache was pounding. There were a few other kids roaming around. Everyone was walking slowly, probably because no one wanted to get where they were going.

Mr. French was setting up some card tables in the quad. He was humming the Wanton Weasels' "Gotcha, Gotcha, by Goodness, I Gotcha."

"It's four hundred dollars to get the window fixed," he said as I passed. "Four hundred dollars!!!"

"Is that my problem?" I asked.

"It is if you mistake a car for a garbage can," he said.

My headache suddenly got worse. Why was I even bothering to talk to Mr. French? Everyone knew he was nuts.

"They have to straighten out the door before they fix the window," he went on.

"That's a shame," I said, trying to get past him.

He stepped in front of me and blocked my way. "You rich kids don't give a damn about anyone or anything but yourselves, do you?"

I made a mental note to cross off Mr. French's name. It cost money to make those flyers. Money he clearly didn't have.

"I'm late," I told him.

Mr. French stepped aside and bowed to me.

I bypassed the nurse's office and headed straight to the admin office. "Principal Kostantino," I shouted over the reception counter.

She didn't seem surprised to see me. "Higgs," she said, letting out a sigh of resignation. "Well, that was unfortunate."

I wasn't sure if she meant me not getting Senior of the Year, or Dinky Dick being broadcast across the school. "Principal Kostantino," I said. "Who is responsible for the —" I didn't want to say it out loud.

"The anatomy announcement?" A bemused smile escaped before she could catch it. "I don't know. Someone hacked into the PA system."

"Well, it's defamation of character," I told her, "and I demand to know who's behind this."

Principal Kostantino was busy going through a pile of papers on Mrs. Sanchez's desk. "I wish I had an answer for you, Higgs," she said. "But I don't. Listen, I know you're upset. But there are only a few more days left of school. Let it go."

Right. Like that was possible.

At lunchtime, the seniors crowded around the folding tables to collect their caps and gowns. I went to A–G.

Rosalee looked up from a sheet of names. "He's in the right line," she told the boy in front of me. "Dinky Dick is between A and G."

A couple of the guys laughed so hard that they almost keeled over.

"Nice to know you know your ABCs," I said gamely.

I had to get out of there.

"I'm sorry, I can't find your form," Samantha Verve said when it was my turn at the front of the table.

"I'm sure it's there," I said evenly.

"Nope," she said, scanning the list again. "No Dinky Dick."

The joke was wearing thin.

Roo came over and sat down next to Samantha. "Maybe I can help," she said. "Because unlike some people, I like to help. What is your last name?"

"You know my last name," I said impatiently.

"Excuse me, but have we met?" Roo said. Her lower lip began to tremble. Tears welled in her light blue eyes. Most people were mesmerized by Roo's eyes. They were like aquamarine gemstones, as flawless and clear as the sky on a perfect day. Only, today was far from perfect.

"Look, I'm sorry —" Before I could finish, Roo's delicate shoulders were heaving as she sobbed.

"Go away!" Samantha shouted, putting a protective arm around Roo.

"Look, I just want my cap and gown," I protested.

Mrs. Sanchez hurried over. "Is there a problem with A through G?" she asked.

"I just want my cap and gown," I pleaded.

Roo and Samantha scowled in solidarity.

"Thank you for the apples, Higgs," Mrs. Sanchez said as she tried to find my order. "I'm going to miss all the fresh fruit! And you too, of course. I'm looking forward to hearing your commencement speech. You've come a long way."

Mrs. Sanchez handed me my cap and gown sealed in a plastic bag, along with a gold tassel for being in the honor society, plus a gold sash with the word "valedictorian" printed on it.

"Thank you," I told her. "For everything."

She nodded. Mrs. Sanchez knew what I meant.

Just then Lauren Fujiyama got in line behind me. It was hard to hate her. Lauren was nice to everyone.

"Hey, congrats," I said.

She smiled shyly. "Thanks, Higgs. It was a huge surprise. I really thought that you were going to get it. Well, you or Zander."

"Well, you can't win them all," I said, trying to smile back. The only thing was, up until that day, I thought I could.

Day 5

CHAPTER 19

My parents were sitting side by side, poring over *Reflections/ snoitcelfeR*. I couldn't recall the last time they'd sat this close to each other.

"It's an odd name, don't you think?" Mom asked.

"snoitcelfeR is Reflections spelled backward," Charlie explained. "And it's not an odd name, it's an incredibly odd and stupid name."

"Twelve! Higgs, you're in here twelve times," Dad crowed. He raised his glass to me.

I still hadn't told him about not getting Senior of the Year. I wasn't sure how he would take that, given that it was the last award Jeffrey had won before heading off to Harvard. Well, wait. Technically, my brother never did go to Harvard. Yes, he was accepted, but he never did make it to his first day of class.

"Thirteen," I corrected my father. "I'm in there thirteen times."

"Very nice," Mom said. "You're very photogenic, honey. Although I wish you had gotten a haircut for your jazz band photo."

"What about me?" Charlie asked. "I'm in there too, you know."

Dad finished off his second Chivas, then swirled the ice around the empty glass. "Charlie, your photo is with all the others in the freshman class section. You're going to need to get more active in school if you want to go to Harvard, like your brother."

"What if I don't want to go to Harvard like my brother?" Charlie snorted. She shoved a handful of Doritos in her mouth and crunched angrily. "Besides, I'm in there more than once."

"Oh! Where?" Mom brightened. "Show me."

"I'm on the music page, plus there," Charlie said, stabbing at a picture with her finger.

"Where?"

"There!"

"That's you?" My mother squinted.

"Uh-huh," Charlie answered. I sensed a twinge of pride in her voice. "I'm a member of the StreetArt Asylum, a.k.a. STartA."

"Shouldn't that be STart Ass?" I said.

Everyone ignored me.

"You're a SweeTart?" asked Mom. "Isn't that a candy?"

"StreetART . . . Street Art . . . ," Charlie tried to explain. "You know, outsider art in the streets."

"Is that safe?" Mom was still examining the photo.

"Let me see that," Dad said, taking the yearbook. "That's not you!"

"It is me, I swear!" Charlie cried. "That's me behind the boy wearing the Andy Warhol wig."

"And how is being in the Sweetheart Club going to help you to get into Harvard?" Dad asked in his I-am-forming-this-as-a-question-but-it's-really-me-telling-you-something way.

I put a pillow over my face to stop from laughing.

"Urrgggg!!!!" Charlie shouted. "Damn all of you, and damn Harvard!"

We sat still and watched her storm out of the room.

"Three . . . two . . . one," I counted down. Right on cue, Charlie ran back in and grabbed the bag of Doritos. Then she stopped, glared at me, and yelled, "Dinky Dick!!!"

My father watched Charlie retreat to her room. "You should talk to her about her language," he said to my mother. "It really is unacceptable."

Mom shook her head. "She's always so angry. I don't know what to do about that girl."

"You could farm her out to another family," I suggested.

Dad chuckled as my mother cautioned me, "Now, Higgs, be nice to your sister. Not everyone has the gifts you have."

Day 5

CHAPTER 20

A skinny slacker dude was manning the cash register. His T-shirt read "I am currently out of the office."

I had stopped at the iffy Mart and picked up a pack of Camel cigarettes, a Butterfinger, and a coffee, black, for myself. I started drinking coffee my freshman year to stay awake. By my senior year, I was a full-fledged caffeine addict.

The water tower loomed in the distance like a lighthouse without a beacon. As I crossed the gravel pit, I wondered why I was ever scared of it. Just then, I spotted a leg sticking up from the dirt. My heart leaped and a scream escaped, until I realized it was just a branch. Behold the power of suggestion.

Even though it was obscured by plants I could still see the rounded roof of the once-silver Airstream trailer. It reminded me of a giant pill bug rising among the weeds. Nick and I used to play with pill bugs when we were kids. They'd be crawling along the sidewalk, and we'd pick them up and watch them curl up in the palms of our hands before putting them back on the ground.

One time when I was little, I accidentally stepped on a pill bug and couldn't stop crying. Later, Jeffrey came up to me with something in his hand. He uncurled his fingers. "See," he said as he tousled my hair with his other hand. "You didn't squish it, it's still alive."

As I got closer, I could see Monarch sitting outside the trailer in her lawn chair.

"Hello!" I called out. I began to jog toward her, then walked in an attempt to dial down my enthusiasm.

"Well, well," Monarch said, lowering her cat's-eye sunglasses and looking at me over the top of *Madame Bovary*. "If it isn't Higgs Boson Bing, the human collider."

Was I blushing? God, I hoped I was not blushing.

I handed her the cigarettes and candy bar.

"Coffee?" she said.

I handed her that too.

Without taking her eyes off of me, Monarch ripped the candy bar wrapper open with her teeth — she had nice teeth, perfectly even and white — and then broke off a piece. After removing the lid of the cup, she dropped the chunk of Butterfinger into the coffee. She put the lid back on, placed her thumb over the opening, and shook it up.

I wasn't sure if Monarch was testing me, flirting with me, or challenging me, so I remained silent. She took a sip of coffee. "Ahhh, that's good stuff," she said, closing her eyes and clearly enjoying herself. I felt like a pervert watching her, but still, I couldn't turn away.

Monarch's skin was pale and smooth, unlike Roo's, who had been known to visit a tanning salon when the sun wasn't cooperating. Monarch's nose was small, but her lips were full. She had on bright red lipstick again. Her eyelids, rimmed with black, set off her hazel-blue eyes, which sparkled like they knew a secret. Roo aspired to be fashion model thin and gave the impression that she could float away at any given time. But Monarch was, and I mean this in the nicest way, grounded.

"What are you staring at?" Monarch asked when the cup was drained.

"Nothing," I said. "Hey, did you get the cigarettes and Butterfinger from yesterday?"

Monarch arched an eyebrow. "Oh, those were from you?"

"Well, yeah, who did —?" Oh. She was making fun of me. When she started laughing, I did too. It was the first time I had laughed in two days.

Monarch had found an old plastic kiddie pool near the car graveyard and made me drag it across the gravel pit and up to her trailer. We were both sitting in it and she was using a broken tennis racket and rowing like she was in a boat. The shade from a giant oak covered us. We'd been there nearly an hour and neither of us had said anything, although every now and then she'd scream something like, "Alligator!" and fight off the imaginary creature with the tennis racket.

I couldn't have spent an hour with Roo without her rambling on and on about some inane topic, like whether she should part her hair in the middle, or if bananas made you fat, or if, when we're married, we'd have one or two kids.

Finally, I said to Monarch, "How long have you been here?"

"Been where?" she asked, staring at a hawk overhead. "In this boat? In the Airstream? In this world?"

"All three, I guess," I said.

Monarch reached down into her boot and retrieved a cherry-red Zippo lighter with a rooster on it, then lit up. She tapped the cigarette ashes into an empty Spam can. I was charmed that we were out in the woods and yet she used an ashtray.

"I have been in this boat to nowhere with Higgs Boson for about an hour?" she said. I had almost forgotten that I had asked her a question. "I don't have a watch," she continued, "so I'm just guessing. It feels like I've been on my own for about forever, and I've been on the planet for eighteen years."

"Me too," I said.

"You're on your own?" For the first time, she looked interested in me.

"No, I'm eighteen too."

"Oh," Monarch said, clearly disappointed.

"All right," I told her. "Now you can ask me three questions about myself."

"What if I don't want to know anything about you?"

"Well, then you don't have to," I said, slightly wounded.

Monarch, rather ungracefully, got out of the rowboat and walked away.

I stayed seated, unsure of what to do.

Finally, she turned around. "Higgs Boson!" Monarch shouted. "Are you coming or not? I've thought of a question."

Day 5

CHAPTER 21

I had to sprint to catch up to Monarch, who was happily tramping through the tall weeds and whacking them with the unstrung tennis racket. She had a pretty good backhand. Monarch was about eight inches shorter than me, but I wouldn't have bet against her in a fight.

As I neared, she turned around and gave me an evil grin before swatting me with the racket.

"Hey," I cried. "That hurt!"

"Why are you here?" Monarch asked, holding the racket as if she meant to hit me again.

"Because you told me to come with you," I reminded her as I rubbed my shoulder. I slowly stepped away from her, lest she attack again.

"No, why are you *here*? That's my question. Why are you in Brookhaven? Why aren't you playing with your after-school friends?"

"School's not going so well right now," I admitted.

"Why?" she asked as we neared a gnarled old tree that seemed to shoot up for miles.

"It's complicated," I answered.

"What grade are you in?"

"Senior. I graduate on Saturday. What about you?"

She started to say something, before stopping herself. I regretted asking the question. Monarch seemed like the drop-outs who hung around campus. My suspicions were confirmed when she said sullenly, "A high school diploma leads to what, Higgs? Another four-year prison term?"

We walked in silence.

"Give me a boost," Monarch ordered when we got to the tree.

As she climbed, I followed, and when I was halfway up, I settled into a sturdy branch and wrapped my arms around the trunk. Monarch kept going higher and I couldn't help but look up her dress. She was wearing black panties. I wondered if her bra was black too? That is, if she was even wearing one.

"Higgs Boson, explain yourself," Monarch demanded.

I started to tell her that I didn't mean to look up her dress, until I realized that wasn't what she was talking about. So instead, I explained the flyers and the PA announcement, and that I didn't get Senior of the Year. It felt so good to finally talk to someone about it all, like a weight had been lifted. I didn't mention Roo or the kidney hypothetical.

The sound began low and worked its way up to full-out howl. Monarch could not, or would not, stop laughing. "That is SO pathetic," she cried. "I LOVE it! You are such a loser!!!"

If I hadn't been sitting in a tree, I would have walked away. Forget Monarch. Who was she anyway? Just some random girl who lived in a trailer in the woods? Who was she to make fun of me — Harvard-bound Higgs Boson Bing, Sally Ride High Valedictorian, Debate Captain, Varsity Track.

"Dinky Dick!" she yelped. "How funny is that?!!!"

By then, she was laughing so hard that no sound came out.

"It's not funny at all," I muttered. "And it's *not* dinky," I added a little louder.

I was glad she was above me and couldn't see my face. My jaw had locked into that painful position that inflicted itself upon my father whenever someone mentioned Trent Tenafly.

"Oh, but it is funny," Monarch insisted.

How long can one person laugh? I wondered.

"It's beyond funny because it's so surreal, like you've been shit on in every direction, and keep popping up for more. You're a shit magnet! Oh, wait, I've got it. You're like those Whac-A-Moles, only instead of getting hit with a mallet, you get shit on!!!"

Monarch climbed down the tree, over me, and then stood below, grinning.

I pretended to be interested in the tree bark.

"Come on." She motioned to me. "Stop feeling sorry for yourself and get down here. Set your worries aside for a while. They'll be there when you get back!"

I shook my head. I wasn't talking to her.

"Oh, Higgs Boson Bing, grow up," Monarch chided. "So you had a bad couple of days. Big deal. It could be a lot worse. You could have actual problems."

I picked at a leaf. There was a spider on it, so I set him gently on a branch.

"Dinky," she called out in a faux sweet voice. Her regular voice radiated confidence, unlike Roo, who made everything sound like a question, or Rosalee, who made everything sound like a command.

"Oh, Dinky, are you having a private moment up there?" Monarch asked.

"Shut up," I muttered.

She pouted. "Now, now, Dinky, is that any way to talk to a friend?"

Then the strangest thing happened — I started to smile. I struggled to tamp it down. My situation was not funny, she was not funny, I reminded myself.

"Dinky . . . ?"

Suddenly, the laughter doubled as I joined in.

"Come on down, Higgs," Monarch said as she bent over to catch her breath.

"I can't," I told her.

"Why?"

"Because," I confessed, "I'm scared."

"Listen," Monarch said. Her head was tilted back as she looked up at me. "Name-calling and not winning an award is nothing to be scared of. Wondering where your next meal is coming from, now that's a problem." Monarch imitated a game show announcer and yelled, "Higgs Boson Bing, come on down!"

"I can't," I insisted.

"Yes, you can."

"No, I can't."

She put her hands on her hips. "What is your problem, Higgs?"

I wrapped my arms tighter around the tree. "I'm scared of heights."

"What? I can't hear you."

"I AM SCARED OF HEIGHTS, OKAY? ARE YOU HAPPY NOW?"

I was sure Monarch was going to start laughing at me again, but she didn't. Instead, she shook her head and walked away, leaving me stuck up a tree.

Day 5

CHAPTER 22

It felt as if I had been perched in that tree forever. I had my cell phone, I could have called someone. But who? Nick couldn't talk to me and Roo wouldn't. My mother would start crying and my father would get mad. Charlie would never let me live it down. What was I doing in a tree, anyway? Trying to pick up some tattooed girl? What was her story? I wondered. Maybe she was a grifter. You know, one of those criminals who scams people.

Great. I was probably stuck in a tree forever, all because of some gritty grifter chick. As I resigned myself to the sad fact that I would probably die in that tree, I heard whistling in the distance. I wasn't sure whether to call out or to be silent.

The sound got louder. Someone was whistling, "Heigh-ho, heigh-ho, off to work we go," from *Snow White*. That was one of Charlie's favorite movies when we were little. She used to cry when I called her Dopey. Only, it wasn't Dopey or any of the dwarfs who was whistling, it was Monarch . . . and she was carrying a ladder!

"I wouldn't do this for just anyone," she said as she heaved it against the trunk of the tree. "But for my favorite Dinky Dick, well . . . I had no choice but to rescue you."

I was embarrassed to admit it, but at that moment, my heart beat faster. She was my knight in shining armor.

Monarch steadied the ladder as I climbed down.

"Careful," she told me. "Some of the steps are missing."

It seemed as if the tree was spinning around like an old-fashioned barber shop pole. Still, I kept going, slowly, slowly, one step at a time. When my feet finally hit the dirt, I leaned over and started to hyperventilate.

I had made it.

Monarch was chewing on a stick, and somehow made this look attractive. She didn't say a word.

"What?" I said, annoyed.

"Nothing," she said. She threw the stick across a bank of weeds. I was impressed by how far it flew. "It's just that your fear of heights amuses me."

"So happy that I can brighten your day," I remarked. While Roo sort of floated when she walked, Monarch clomped like she was killing cockroaches.

"I'm on the track team," I offered up as evidence of my manliness. "Varsity."

"Oh yeah, in what?"

"High jump."

Monarch snorted again.

"What now?"

"Well, you're scared of heights and yet you do the high jump? Aren't you a sweet little package of contradiction?"

There was some irony in that, I had to admit.

"So what are you afraid of?" I asked.

She got quiet as her walk slowed. I wondered if I had overstepped my boundaries.

"Do you have parents?"

She shrugged.

"What do you do for food? For money?" I pressed.

Suddenly, things didn't seem so funny to her.

"Look, Mr. Bing," Monarch stopped walking. I felt like a Dinky Dick for getting so personal. "What I do is my business," she said matter-of-factly. "Anything I tell you has to be kept secret. If you're going to be my friend, you have to respect that, okay?"

I felt warm inside. She called me her friend.

I nodded. "Okay."

Monarch smiled. Her smile could light up a room. Oh, shit. I was starting to sound like a greeting card, or Roo.

"I haven't done this with many people," Monarch said, moving closer to me. My breathing quickened. Slowly, she unfastened the silver safety pin that kept the top of her dress together.

Her bra was black.

I could hardly breathe.

"Higgs," she said, leaning in to me.

"Yes," I whispered.

"Give me your hand."

I blinked back my surprise. Most girls waited for you to make the first move. I'd never been with someone like this before. I liked it.

I placed my hand in hers and she drew it toward her breast as she stared into my eyes.

"OUCH!" I screamed. "What did you do that for?"

"To get the blood," Monarch said, like I'd asked a stupid question.

What???

"Goddamn it," I yelled, yanking my hand back. "What are you, some sort of vampire or something?"

"A vampire?" she barked. "Hardly."

With that, she stabbed her own finger with the safety pin. Even though it was little more than a tiny drop, the sight of blood made me feel faint. "If we're going to swear to keep each other's secrets," Monarch explained, "we need to do it with blood to make it official."

That was some crazy shit. That girl was crazy.

"Come on," Monarch insisted, lowering her raspy voice to a whisper. "Hold your hand up like this." When I hesitated, she said, "Higgs, do it."

Begrudgingly, I mimicked her. She pressed our two bleeding fingers together, then wrapped her free hand around ours, bonding them together.

"Repeat after me," Monarch ordered. "I, Higgs Boson Bing . . ."

When I didn't do it right away, she stomped on my foot. "Ouch! Okay, okay. I, Higgs Boson Bing . . ."

"Do solemnly swear . . ."

"Do solemnly swear," I repeated.

"To keep Monarch's secrets a secret."

"To keep Monarch's secrets a secret."

"Good boy," she said.

"Whoa, wait," I told her. "Your turn. Repeat after me. I, Monarch — do you have a last name?" I asked.

She shook her head.

"Okay," I continued, "I, Monarch, do solemnly swear to keep Higgs Boson Bing's secrets a secret."

"I, Monarch, do solemnly swear to keep Higgs Boson Bing's secrets a secret."

When we were done, it felt like something serious had passed between us. I stepped forward to kiss her, but before I could, Monarch started spinning. Her dress flared out around her.

"Hey, Higgs Boson, wanna see something great?" She didn't wait for my answer. "Follow me!"

Monarch had a good head start, but I was fast. When I caught up to her, I jogged backward as she ran forward. She was in pretty good shape for a smoker.

"Where are we going?" I asked. My finger still hurt where she stabbed it.

"You'll see," Monarch said as she slowed.

We walked in silence, again. I liked that. She was the anti-Roo. Still, there were so many things I wanted to ask Monarch, but I was almost afraid that if I pressed too hard, she'd disappear and I'd realize that I had only imagined her.

Monarch stopped abruptly. Her face lit up and I followed her gaze. There, in the clearing, was a small patch of vibrant colors surrounded by a ring of trees.

"Those are mine," she said almost reverently.

"The trees?"

"No, the flowers. The flowers! Look at the flowers."

"Beautiful," I said, not taking my eyes off of her. I turned to Monarch's flowers. "How are these yours?"

"Squatter's rights," she said.

"So, what are you going to do with this?" I asked as she took my hand and pulled me into the center of the field.

Monarch looked puzzled. "What do you mean?" She picked a daisy and put it in her hair, then reached over to put a pink flower in mine. I didn't stop her.

"Are you going to sell the flowers?"

"No," she said, sounding insulted. "This is a gift from Mother Nature."

"But you could make money," I told her. "You could sell the flowers and buy stuff —"

"Higgs, I've got things to do," Monarch said suddenly. "You have to go now."

I'd blown it.

"Okay, yeah. Me too." I told her. "Will you be here tomorrow?"

"One never knows," she said.

Then Monarch disappeared, leaving me alone in a field of flowers with a bleeding finger and unanswered questions.

Wednesday

Day 4

CHAPTER 23

Y ou would have thought the amusement factor I provided would have diminished by Wednesday. Not so. I was still hearing a smattering of "Dinky Dick" as I cleared out my locker. Plus, I was no longer "Higgs Bing, Valedictorian, Harvard," but had morphed into "the jerk who broke poor Roo's heart." Not that it mattered that technically she was the one who broke up with me. Over a HYPOTHETICAL.

What few knew about Rosemary "Roo" Wynn was that her bubbly personality masked a clingy, needy, and high-maintenance girlfriend. If I didn't tell Roo how pretty she was at least three times a day, she'd actually start to wither. Seriously. Roo would get all pouty and then she'd hunch over and say, "Higgs, don't you find me attractive anymore?"

To which, I was to reply, "Really, Roo, how can you say that? You are the most beautiful girl at Sally Ride."

What Roo liked about me, she often said, was that I was steady and had a good future. "Fashion changes, music changes, but you, Higgs, don't. With you I know exactly what I'm getting."

At first, I was insulted. Then I realized, that was why I was with Roo. I knew exactly what I was getting. My life was so hyperfocused on getting into Harvard, a school whose name gave a person instant credibility and confidence, that I didn't have time to deal with the unknown. Dating around would have derailed me. I was comfortable with Roo.

When I spotted Nick near the cafeteria, I instinctively headed toward him. I wanted to tell him about Monarch. "You are not going to believe this," I began.

Before I could get any farther, Samantha grabbed his arm and whispered something in his ear. Nick nodded and offered an apologetic shrug before leaving with her.

Okay. Okay, Nicholas Milgram, I thought, if that's how you want to play it, I can do that too. Forget that we were ever best friends. "Screw you," I muttered as I strode past him. Nick started to say something, but Samantha shushed him.

My cell phone vibrated. There was a text from my father. Call me, it read. Before I could hit delete, the phone rang. It was Dad.

"Who died?" I asked, panicked.

"No one died," he said solemnly. "But I have bad news. Harvard called. They said they're reevaluating your application."

I wasn't sure if I had heard correctly. "What was that?"

"They're looking at your public service record and feel that you may have misrepresented yourself. It's probably no big deal. They got an anonymous call —"

I didn't hear the rest of what he was saying.

I texted Nick. Call me. It's important, I swear.

Almost before I finished, the phone rang. It was Nick.

"Holy crap!" he shouted when I told him. It felt great that we were both on the same side again, even if we were looking at each other from opposite ends of the cafeteria.

"Who would turn you in?" he asked. "Who would do something like that?"

"A Dinky Dick," I answered.

"I'll bet it was Rosalee," he said. "She hates you."

"Really?" I answered sarcastically "You think so? Hey, Nick, you didn't put SAP on your USC application, did you?"

"No, I thought we were just doing it for Sally Ride Helps Week." I could hear Samantha yapping in the background. "I'll explain later," he told her. "Higgs, I thought you were crazy to put it on your Harvard application. Samantha said it was a death wish."

"You told Samantha?"

"Well, yeah, I tell her everything."

I shook my head. "Christ, Nick. It was probably her."

Now it was his turn to shake his head. "She wouldn't do that," he said.

"Does she tell *you* everything?" I asked.

"Lay off her, Higgs," he warned. "She's my fiancée."

The warning bell rang and students headed to their classes. No one rushed. It was, after all, the last week of school.

Rosalee Gomez was watching me. She had a smug smile on her face. "Are you happy now?" I shouted.

By then, she was across the courtyard. She let go of a loud laugh that sounded like it was in an echo chamber. Everything seemed surreal. Mr. Avis was spying on me from his office. Even though he was inside, I could hear him laughing too. I was having trouble standing. It felt like the earth had slipped off its axis.

In the distance, Lauren Fujiyama was with Roo — when had they ever been friends? I wondered. They linked arms as they skipped in slow motion toward Nick and Samantha Verve, who were chanting, "Moral compass, moral compass . . ." Their voices echoed loudly and were slurred and deep. Zander Findley was playing the drums as Mr. French swept the quad, even though it was spotless. Wayward Hitler Higgs flyers whirled around me as if I were in the center of a cyclone.

I started to run and knocked down several students. As I stumbled, I could hear them yelling at me, only it sounded like we were underwater, and I was drowning.

Day 4

CHAPTER 24

I splashed more water on my face. Rehearsals were already under way and I was late. Mr. Avis glared at me as I ran onto the field like a forgotten football player. I had been hiding in the boys' bathroom, the grossest place in the universe — that's how badly I needed to be alone.

Mr. Hermes had his eyes closed as he led the band in "Pomp and Circumstance." I could see Charlie with her cello leaned up against her like a shield. The senior class marched single file up to the giant X on the field, then split off with every other person going to the left and to the right. It shouldn't have been complicated, but it was. Students were colliding like bumper cars. So much for the future leaders of tomorrow.

I said hi to Libby Bukowski as she let me cut in front of her. Libby was going to CalArts and Charlie was always talking about "Libby this," and "Libby that." Libby was SRHS's resident bohemian artist and often wore tiny hats perched at odd angles on her head.

"People . . . people, pay attention," Mr. Avis barked into the microphone. "If the person in front of you goes left, you go right. GOT IT???" I almost felt sorry for him, until he added, "Thank you to everyone who managed to get here on time." I could feel him smirking. "Commencement speakers, Zander Findley, Higgs Bing, and Lauren Fujiyama, as you march forward, instead of sitting with the rest of the senior class, you three will veer off and sit on the stage with Principal Kostantino and me."

My father's phone call was still ringing in my ears.

As Mr. Avis droned on about the importance of getting to graduation "on time, everyone," I scrutinized my fellow seniors. Some were sitting rapt and listening to Mr. Avis. Lauren Fujiyama was even taking notes. Others were goofing off. Quite a few were texting, and a couple of the stoners were sleeping.

One by one, I searched out the people on my list. Roo spotted me looking at her, and stuck out her tongue. Samantha was examining her fingernails. Zander Findley looked bored. Rosalee Gomez was staring right back at me. But where was Nick? I didn't see Nick.

Just then the Talky Boys' one hit, "Heartless Empty-Hearted Heartbreaker," blasted over the loudspeakers.

You, you ripped my soul apart
You, you are without a heart

"Can someone turn that off?" Mr. Avis shouted.

The song stopped abruptly, and an all-too-familiar digitized voice said, "We interrupt our musical interlude to bring you a special announcement. . . . Extensive studies have revealed that Higgs Boson Bing is a Dinky Dick."

Again? Seriously? Again?

It wasn't funny the first time, and it sure as hell wasn't funny that time — but try telling that to the 398 graduating seniors. They were howling. I stood up and took a bow, when really I wanted to destroy every single person who was laughing at me.

"Sit down, Mr. Bing," Mr. Avis said. His head looked like it was about to explode. "Seniors, calm down."

It took a while to get everyone to shut up, especially when some of the stoners started a "Dinky Dick" chant. I knew one thing for sure — when I found out who was behind it all, I was going to make their life hell.

Day 4

CHAPTER 25

I'm sorry, Jeffrey," my mother was saying. "But this is for the best."

"Hey, Mom," I said as I headed to the kitchen. I threw my backpack down. I'm not sure why I still carried it when we had no work the last week of school. Habit, I guess.

"How was graduation practice?" she asked. Her back was to me as she stood at the fireplace mantel.

I hesitated. Do I tell her that my life is unraveling? I wondered. That some sort of psychopath had me on their hit list, and that the entire school was turning against me? I still hadn't told my parents that I didn't get Senior of the Year, and I sure as hell wasn't about to tell them about the girl in the woods.

"Fine," I said. "You look nice."

She was wearing her orange dress and there was no sign of the Robe of Depression.

"Thank you, Higgs. I had lunch with your father," she said by way of explanation.

From the way she was acting, it was clear she didn't know about my Harvard application. I was surprised my father hadn't mentioned it. I started to tell her, but thought that it could wait. She seemed distracted. Well, more distracted than usual.

There were no potato chips in the cupboard, so I grabbed a box of my mother's ThinCrisp crackers and popped one into my mouth. It tasted bland. Thin and crispy, but bland.

Mom came up and hugged me. Did she know? Maybe Dad told her after all. She didn't let me go for a long time, and that was when I noticed she was crying.

"Mom?"

She wiped away her tears. "It's nothing," she said, fixing a smile to her face. "I'll be fine. We'll be fine. Everything will be fine. It's for the best. Trust me."

My mother continued to cry as she rewashed the dishes. I wandered into the living room. Charlie was curled up on the couch. She had aimed the remote at the television and was changing channels nonstop. I was about to swat her with a pillow, when she looked up at me. Her eyes were all red. She'd been crying too.

"Did she tell you?" Charlie asked.

"Who? Did who tell me what?"

"Dad's moving out. Mom and Dad are splitting up."

I couldn't breathe. I sank into the couch next to Charlie. She stared crying again, only no sound was coming out. I hesitated, then put my arm around her. I could see Mom standing in the doorway, watching us. Even in the Robe of Depression, I'd never seen her look so sad. Well, only once before.

"Mom?"

She didn't respond, but instead just stood frozen like she was in her own world.

Why was he doing this? I wondered. Was it Mrs. Taelo? Maya Taelo was always flirting with my father. She even used to tease Mom. *"Elizabeth, if you ever get tired of this man, give him to me."*

My mother gripped her stomach as if she was in severe pain. Charlie looked as worried as I was. For once, I was glad that my sister was there.

"Mom?"

"It's for the best," she said again, sounding unconvinced.

"Are you going to be okay?"

"This has been coming for a long time," she struggled to explain.

I used to feel sorry for Nick because his parents were divorced. When he was little, they'd shuttle him back and forth, and his mom and dad were always fighting over him. It was never truly about him, Nick claimed. It was about them, and who won and who lost. In a weird way, Nick said, he liked that they were fighting because, "At least that means they're talking."

My parents had stopped talking years ago.

Oh sure, they bickered all the time, over stupid stuff, like whose turn it was to empty the dishwasher, or whether to get unleaded supreme gas (Dad) or regular unleaded (Mom). However, when it came to me, they were a united front. Harvard. It was always Harvard. I knew that if I could get into Harvard, I could make them both happy. But there I was, heading to Harvard, and now they weren't speaking to each other. They weren't even going to live together anymore. Maybe getting me into Harvard was what had been keeping them together.

"Charlie will live with me," my mother was saying. How long had she been talking?

I nodded. Charlie made a wailing sound and clutched a pillow. Mom went to hug her, but my sister batted her away.

"Do you still love him?" I asked.

"No matter what happens between us, we will always be your parents — we have that in common," she said, not answering my question. "And we have you and Charlie."

And Jeffrey, I wanted to add. *There was Jeffrey too.* But I didn't say anything. My mother was sad enough as it was.

Day 4

CHAPTER 26

My stomach churned. I could hear my father's Porsche pulling into the driveway. I braced myself knowing that what had been a shitty day was going to get a whole lot shittier. From the kitchen, I strained to hear my parents talking. No voices were raised, but there was a definite hum of deep discord punctuated by my mother crying, "No, that's not possible!"

Could he hurt her even more?

"Higgs?" My father summoned me to the living room.

Mom was on the couch, staring at Jeffrey's photo and absent-mindedly shredding a tissue. My father was in his leather chair, still wearing his white dentist jacket. There was a smudge of red on it. Blood? Lipstick? Even though it was early afternoon, he was holding his beloved Chivas on the rocks.

"Higgs" — my mother's voice sounded thin — "your father has informed me that Harvard is reevaluating your application. Is there something you'd like to say?"

"Why are you separating?" I asked. "Are you getting a divorce?"

My parents glanced uncomfortably at each other.

"No, no divorce," Dad finally said, clearing his throat. "We're just taking a little break from each other, isn't that right, Elizabeth?" When she didn't answer, he repeated himself, only louder. "Isn't that right, Elizabeth?"

What an asshole.

Mom nodded. She looked tired.

"Higgs," my father said, "was this SAP — this Society of Animal Protection whatever thing you set up legit?"

I shrugged. "We saved a dog."

"I see," Dad said. "Higgs, this could be serious."

My throat went dry. "How serious?"

"They could withdraw your invitation to Harvard."

A cold panic overtook me. I sunk into the couch.

My father tossed back his drink and set the glass down on the coffee table. Mom picked it up as if it were toxic and placed a coaster under it.

"I'm sure we'll get through this," Dad said in his take-charge voice. "We just need to prove it was real. That should be easy enough."

"Do you have paperwork on it? Something to prove that it was real?" Mom asked. "Where is that dog you rescued now?"

"With Nick," I said.

She nodded. "Good. Nick took him in."

Technically, she was correct.

"I'll talk to John Dullaghan," my father interrupted. "John's a Harvard grad and a corporate lawyer. I just pulled his wisdom teeth — they were impacted at an odd angle. He may be able to advise us."

"Advise us for what?" Mom asked. "Higgs did nothing wrong. If anything, he should be praised for helping that poor dog and finding it a home."

I could see how easy it would have been for Dad to scam her all these years. For someone so incredibly smart, my mother could be very naive. I could hardly look at my father. Suddenly, all those late night meetings made sense.

"Higgs, this is no joke. This is real serious stuff," Dad said sharply.

I stopped smirking and nodded. We all knew how he felt about his alma mater. Jeffrey was the one who was supposed to graduate from Harvard with a DDS and then go into the family business. Nothing could stop him from fulfilling my father's dream. Well, nothing but a bottle of Chivas, a streetlight, and a Toyota Corolla going 85 miles per hour in a 30 miles-per-hour zone.

"Elizabeth," he said to Mom, "I'm going to get some of my things and I'll go to a hotel tonight."

Dad waited for her to say something, but when she didn't, he got up and retreated to his den. That's when Mom burst into tears. I never knew what I was supposed to do when my mother was crying. At least she wasn't in her Robe of Depression. I hated that robe.

All of a sudden I saw Charlie lingering in the hallway like a misplaced shadow. I motioned for my sister to come in, and when she did, she went right over to Mom and gave her a hug. Then they both started crying. Mom with her familiar soft sobs, Charlie with a deep animal-like wail. It was like a cacophony of pain.

I needed to get away.

Day 4

CHAPTER 27

Please, please, please let her be home.

My chest was on fire, but I didn't stop until I reached the Airstream. If I were running the 880, I would have broken the school record. I banged on the door with both fists. "Monarch? Monarch, I need to talk to you!"

There was no answer. Sweat was dripping down my face. I pulled the door open. No Monarch.

I ran to her flower field.

She wasn't there either.

I checked the climbing tree, the car graveyard. Everywhere. But she was nowhere. I headed back to the Airstream to wait.

I wondered what was going to happen? My dad was moving out. Did that mean my parents were divorcing? Was I going to get nailed by Harvard? Who snitched on me? Suddenly, being called a Dinky Dick seemed quaint.

"Monarch!" I yelled.

In the distance, Monarch was striding toward me, oblivious to my pain. As soon as I saw her, I felt relief wash over me and I was able to breathe.

Monarch didn't look surprised to see me, and I tried to play it cool, but my heart was racing. I wasn't sure if it was the proximity to her or my crumbling life that was causing the palpitations. In lieu of a hello, I handed her a bag from Benny's B-Burgers, a gift I thought she would appreciate. Nick had worked there until a couple of months earlier when he got busted for charging four dollars to deep-fry anything anyone brought in. Most people brought Twinkies and candy bars, that sort of stuff. But when Archie Kunda gave him an old CD player, it messed up the deep fryer and Nick got fired.

Monarch rummaged through the bag, handed me the hamburger, and devoured the fries, eating several at a time.

"Don't you want the burger?" I asked.

"I'm a vegetarian," Monarch informed me. She eyed the chocolate shake still in my hands.

"So, um, what were you doing?" I said. Just standing near her was comforting.

Monarch held up a book. *Arthur Rimbaud: Complete Works.*

"Ah, good old Rimbaud," I said knowingly. "I love his later stuff."

"You've never read Rimbaud, have you, Higgs?"

I shook my head.

"Try expanding your horizons now and then," Monarch said, "and read something other than what's on the AP reading list or Vonnegut."

"How did you know I read Vonnegut?" I asked, surprised.

"You reek of the type," she said as she checked the bag for more fries.

I should have gotten the super size. I made a mental note to do that next time.

"Have you read Vonnegut?" I asked, glancing over her shoulder at her small pile of books.

"'I can have oodles of charm when I want to,'" Monarch said, quoting him.

"*Cat's Cradle*," I told her.

"*Breakfast of Champions*," she corrected me.

"May I come in?" I asked. We were both still standing in the doorway.

"It's not big enough for two," she said.

I didn't move.

"Is that for me?" Monarch asked, motioning to the chocolate shake.

"It is if you let me in," I said, taking a long protracted sip.

Monarch took the shake and stepped aside. "Come on in, Higgs." She released a heavy sigh. "But you're going to have to crouch."

I hoped she couldn't see my face, since I was grinning like a kid who had won the giant giraffe at a carnival.

There was hardly room for two — plus, being that close to Monarch was making me anxious. I wanted to jump, or run, or pace, or something, but there wasn't enough room. So instead, I devoured the hamburger as Monarch looked on in disgust.

"I wath hungry," I said with my mouth full. Actually, I was starving. Stress did that to me.

Monarch was sitting cross-legged and her dress rose above

her knees. When she saw me staring at her legs, she slammed Rimbaud shut without bothering to use a bookmark and adjusted her hem. "Okay, Higgs, spill," she ordered. She removed the lid from the shake and took a big swig. "Spill," Monarch said again, looking deadly serious, despite a chocolate shake mustache. "I can tell you have something to say."

"My dad's moving out," I told her. I found myself pacing, hunched over in the Airstream. I could only take one step in each direction, so it was like doing the box step with myself. "My sister, Charlie, says she's seen it coming for months, years even, and accused me of being too self-centered to even take note —"

I stopped and I waited for Monarch to make fun of me or tell me to stop feeling sorry for myself, but instead, she said, "I need a cigarette. Let's go outside. I can't smoke in this firetrap."

It was dusk and the air was still. I swatted away a mosquito. In a single move, Monarch flicked open her lighter and produced a flame. I almost reminded her that cigarettes would stain her teeth, but stopped myself. I wasn't there to advocate for good dental hygiene.

"I'm sorry about your parents," Monarch said as we walked up the path. "It sucks when people can't get along." There was no condemnation or sarcasm in her voice. Instead, there was a hint of sadness.

We kept going, the only sound being the occasional call of a bird or the crush of leaves underfoot. Despite whatever had been happening at home, I had never felt so at peace as I did with Monarch right then. I kept stealing glances at her. Monarch looked beautiful bathed in the soft glow of the setting sun. At the thought of what I was about to do next, my heart beat faster. I took a deep breath to fortify myself.

As if she knew, Monarch stopped walking and turned toward me. She tilted her head up to mine and said in her deep, smoky voice, "I don't care how sad you are. Don't put the moves on me, Higgs."

"I . . . I wasn't going to put the moves on you," I sputtered.

"Liar," she said as she continued tromping through the woods. "Get this into that over-analytical brain of yours — hanky-panky is off-limits."

"Hanky-panky?" I asked. "Who says 'hanky-panky'?"

"I say it," she replied.

"What's wrong with hanky-panky?"

"There's nothing wrong with it, when it's with the right person," Monarch said. "But you, Higgs Boson Bing, are not the right person."

It felt like she had kicked me in the gut. But I wasn't about to let her know that. Instead, I asked, "Who is the right person?"

Without breaking her step, Monarch answered, "I'll know when I find him."

I shook off her cavalier dismissal of me. Right then, I needed someone to talk to more than someone to hanky-panky with. "There's more shit going down in my life right now. Harvard is reevaluating my application and may expel me before I start."

When Monarch looked momentarily surprised, I felt a perverse sense of pride that I was able to catch her off guard.

"Hey Higgs," she said. "I'm sorry."

It sounded like she meant it.

"For which one?" I asked. "My parents splitting or my Harvard career being derailed?"

"Which one hurts most?"

I shrugged. "Both are no big deal."

"Man, you're a shitty liar," she said, taking my hand and leading me up the hill. "Come on, let's go."

Our fingers laced up perfectly.

I wasn't sure where Monarch was leading me, and I didn't care. We kept climbing and my phone buzzed repeatedly, but I ignored it. I didn't want to let go of her hand. When we finally stopped, Monarch released me and I felt unmoored. Then I looked around. It was amazing. I could see the high school and downtown. I could see my house — it looked so small. I wished I could see inside. I wondered if my father was still there. I wondered if he and my mother were fighting. I wondered why he was leaving.

"If you think things look great from here," Monarch said, "you ought to see the view from up there." She motioned to the top of the water tower. A rusted chain-link fence topped with barbed wire encircled it. Someone had cut a hole in the fence.

I had to laugh. There was no way in hell that I'd ever go up there. She knew that.

"Monarch," I ventured. "You know all about me, but I don't know anything about you."

"Maybe there's a reason for that," she said, lowering her voice. "Secrets one would rather not have revealed."

I looked at where she pricked my finger. There was no scar, like nothing had ever happened. I almost wished there was something there.

"I won't spill your secrets," I said.

"Tell you what, Higgs, since you're graduating soon, I'm going to give you a present." Monarch leaned in toward me. Our faces were so close that I could almost count her eyelashes. I was ready to kiss her, but she pulled back and said, "You may ask me one question. We'll call it a *bonus question*, because no matter what, I'll have to answer it."

"That's the present?"

"Is that your bonus question?"

I shook my head. "Do I have to ask it right now?"

"Is that your bonus question?"

She wasn't going to make it easy. "Okay," I said. "When I ask it, I'll say, 'Monarch, this is my bonus question.'"

A slow grin crossed her face. "Now you've got it, Higgs Boson Bing. You're learning."

In debate, we asked things rapid-fire, and answered the same. Half the time we were just trying to confuse our opponents. The other half of the time we didn't really want to hear the answers to our questions, we were just throwing the other team off base. This was different. I wasn't about to waste my bonus question.

The hike down the hill wasn't nearly as fun as it was going up. We weren't holding hands this time, and it was getting dark and hard to see.

"Hungry?" Monarch asked as we crossed the gravel pit and headed out of Brookhaven.

"A little," I said.

"Then let's grab dinner. My treat."

I hesitated. I had never thought about it before, but Monarch probably didn't have much money, if any.

"I can't let you do that," I insisted. "Let me buy you dinner."

"That's sweet, Higgs. But don't worry, it's not going to cost anything. You've got a car, right?"

Hesitantly, I nodded. "I'm parked at the iffy Mart."

"Well then, let's go!" she shouted, and then let out a whoop.

"That's your car?"

I had never been more embarrassed to drive a bright red Volvo station wagon than at that moment. The silver BMW with the lawyer bumper sticker was back, and I wished that was my car instead.

"Can I drive?" Monarch asked.

"I don't know if that's a good idea. . . ."

"Oh, please, Higgs. I'm a safe driver, I promise." She was only inches away from me. "Please," she said softly, leaning into me.

I wondered if she could hear my heart racing?

"Say yes, Higgs," Monarch whispered again, playing with my collar and pulling me close.

I could feel her breath. Did she mean for her lips to touch my ear?

"Okay," I said weakly. "But you have to drive safe, promise me."

Monarch broke into a huge grin. "I promise!"

Even though I knew better, I handed her the keys. Delighted, Monarch slipped into the driver's seat and took her time adjusting it. She checked her teeth in the mirror, then ran her hands around the steering wheel. Gingerly, Monarch put Rolvo in reverse and slowly backed out, before hitting the gas.

"Shit! Slow down, stop it!!!" I screamed.

"*Viva la Grand Prix!*" Monarch shouted as I gripped the dashboard.

"SLOW DOWN!!!" I cried. "NOW, GODDAMN IT!!! Are you trying to get us killed?"

By the time we got to the highway, I was exhausted from screaming. Monarch finally slowed and began driving like a normal person. I took deep cleansing breaths in an attempt to regain my composure.

"Christ, Higgs," she said. "Don't crap in your pants, what's the big deal?"

Jeffrey.

"Forget it," I said. "Just, just drive carefully, okay? I can't . . . I can't talk about it."

I rolled down the window to get fresh air.

"Sure, okay," Monarch said, shaking her head. "Sorry."

She kept one hand on the wheel as she rooted around her purse with the other. I watched as she stuck a cigarette in her mouth.

"Where are we going?" I asked. I was back to breathing normal.

"To eat," Monarch said. "There's a place I've always wanted to try." She used the blinker, even as she wove in and out of traffic.

A guy in a black SUV pulled up next to us at the red light. He was wearing sunglasses even though it was dark, but took them off to get a better look at Monarch. When he winked at her, she smiled sweetly before giving him the finger.

"BITCH!" he yelled.

"You're the bitch," Monarch shouted gleefully as the light turned green and she sped away.

I had no idea that Rolvo could go that fast. As soon as it was clear that we had eluded Mr. Sunglasses, I said, "You can slow down now. Please. Please slow down."

Monarch pulled into a strip mall parking lot. Sorrento's Italian restaurant stood next door to a Value Save grocery store.

"Have you ever been here before?" she asked.

"No."

"Do you know anyone who lives near here?"

"No."

"Okay, let's eat!"

Day 4

CHAPTER 28

The restaurant was only half full. White tablecloths, candles. Monarch couldn't decide between two entrées, vegetarian lasagna and a three-cheese calzone, so she got both. I got the spaghetti. She tried ordering a glass of wine.

"I'm sorry, if you don't have proper ID, I can't serve you any alcohol," the waitress said to an unhappy Monarch.

"But in France everyone drinks," Monarch argued.

The waitress smiled wearily. "I wish we were in France, but we're not."

"So tell me more about your parents," Monarch said later as she poured an endless amount of sugar into her iced tea.

"My dad's a dentist," I told her.

"A dentist?" she said.

"There's nothing wrong with being a dentist," I said defensively. "He's pretty successful. He has four offices. He wants me to join his dental practice."

"Do you want to?"

"Why wouldn't I?"

"You didn't answer my question," she said. "Do you want to?"

I hesitated. "I'm not sure," I heard myself saying. "If I didn't become a dentist, my mom and dad would be devastated."

"You're avoiding my question," Monarch pointed out. Was I? "Nothing like a little parental pressure," she continued matter-of-factly. "As I see it, you bend to their will, spend a lifetime doing something you hate, become miserable, and then force your own son or daughter to follow in the family footsteps."

Through two straws, Monarch took a long sip of her iced tea. "But enough about the joys of dentistry," she said. "What about your mother — is she a dentist too? Don't tell me this is a family thing? That would be double the pressure. And if your grand-parents were dentists, that would be a goddamn dental dynasty."

"My grandfather was a dentist," I admitted. I reached for a breadstick and held it like a cigarette. "My mom was a scientist at JPL, Jet Propulsion Lab, but quit to stay home with my sister and me."

"Will she go back to work now that you're heading off to college?"

I had never thought to ask her.

Monarch took my silence to mean something else. "Oh, that's right," she said. "You're not going to Harvard."

"Thanks for reminding me." I broke the breadstick in half and chewed on it.

After dinner, the waitress, who was not that much older than us, came to the table. "Is there anything else I can get for you?" she said, setting down the check.

"Can we have some to-go boxes?" Monarch asked.

As she went to get boxes, Monarch reached toward the check. I put my hand over hers. "I'll get this," I told her.

"I said that dinner would be on me," she reminded me.

The waitress came back with empty containers, which Monarch filled, even taking all the bread from the basket. I watched her slip the salt and pepper shakers into her big purse and a fork and knife too.

While the waitress was busy taking an order on the other side of the room, Monarch leaned in and whispered, "We're going to make a run for it."

"But you haven't paid yet —"

"What? You suddenly got morals?" she asked.

I bristled. "I don't know what you're talking about."

"What exactly did you do to raise Harvard's suspicion?" Monarch's eyes flicked mischievously. She lowered her voice. "Higgs, were you a naughty boy?"

"It's not like anyone was hurt," I insisted.

As I explained the Society for Animal Protection, I felt as if I was at confession and Monarch was the priest. Only, when I was done, instead of absolving me, she declared, "Goddamn, Higgs Boson Bing, you're gonna burn in hell!"

Monarch held the flame in front of my face. I stared at the rooster on the lighter before pushing her hand away. "Gee, thanks for the reassuring words."

"You cheated on your Harvard application, and don't see anything wrong with that. Double standard, Mr. Bing?"

I shook my head. "No, the Harvard thing was different. I would have gotten in even if I hadn't sent the video."

"Then why did you include it?"

I shrugged. "I didn't think I'd get caught," I answered, though it came out more like a question.

Why did I include it? I wondered.

"Anyway, that's apples and oranges," I said. "If we leave here without paying, it's stealing."

Monarch's eyes flashed. "I don't believe you. You are such a hypocrite. What, do you have a sliding scale of right and wrong?"

Why did I include SAP? It made no sense.

Monarch was waiting for an answer.

"I . . . I . . . Look," I said, trying to focus on dinner. "If not paying is about the money, I have money," I told her. "Just let me pay."

"This isn't about the money," Monarch said. "It's about whether or not you have the guts."

"The guts to what?" I asked. "Break the law? Screw the restaurant over?"

The guts to see if I could get away with SAP? Was that it?

"The guts to not do what's expected of you. To live on the edge. To be a rebel, Higgs." Monarch gave me a sly smile. "I gotta admit, I sort of admire that you put that SAP thing on your application."

"You do?"

"HELL yeah! Damn, Higgs. It was like you were giving the finger to the whole Ivy League thing," she said, smiling. "You're more of a man than I thought you were. So then, shall we continue your rebel streak and flee this place?"

I had never dined and dashed before. Nick had told me that when people skipped out on paying their bills at B-Burger, the money came out of the wages of the people who worked there. I was torn between impressing Monarch, who didn't seem to have a problem with screwing the restaurant over, or doing the right thing.

Monarch looked pleased with herself, like the cat that caught a mouse.

"Okay, here's how we will do it," she said, looking around to make sure no one was listening. "I'll get up and pretend that I'm going to the bathroom, when really, I'll slip out the back door. Give me five minutes. After that, you get up — be sure to take the to-go containers — and just walk out the front door. I'll be waiting for you in the car.

"The key here is to act perfectly normal," she instructed me. "When you act like you know what you are doing, people will believe anything. You'd be surprised. If we get stopped, each of us will pretend we thought the other person had paid. You got it?"

I nodded. I felt ill, and wasn't sure if it was because of what I was about to do with Monarch, or because of what I did with SAP.

Monarch's eyes lit up in anticipation. She looked absolutely radiant. "Let's do this!" she whispered as she rose and headed to the back of the restaurant.

Day 4

CHAPTER 29

I rushed out the front door and hurled myself into Rolvo.

"We did it!" Monarch cried gleefully as she threw the car into drive. "Wasn't that fun?"

The truth was, it wasn't fun at all. It was so painful I began to break out in hives. I was about to get up and make a clean getaway, when the waitress headed toward my table. "Is there anything else I can get for you?" she asked.

"No, I'm fine," I lied.

I wondered what Monarch would say if she knew that I paid the bill, then, out of guilt, left a 30 percent tip, plus a couple of extra dollars to cover the salt and pepper shakers and the silverware.

"So Higgs, you appear to have a criminal streak," Monarch said approvingly. "Maybe you can become a con man now that you're not going to college. What is college good for anyway? Hey, I know! We can get the two-for-one special diploma for Dine 'n' Dash. I'll bet Harvard doesn't offer that."

"Just because they're reevaluating my application doesn't mean I'm not going there," I said weakly.

"Let's think about this," Monarch said, suddenly looking pensive. "Maybe there was another student who didn't lie, but didn't get in because you took their place. Maybe you took their place because your daddy pulled some strings. But maybe another student would have gone on to cure cancer or stop the wars, or fix global warming, but since they didn't get into Harvard, they got all depressed and just sat on their couch and watched TV and ate chips, and this caused them to have high cholesterol and gave them an early heart attack, and they died young. Have you considered that, Higgs?"

"Someone might die because I exaggerated?"

"You bet," she said, crossing herself the way Nick used to before every debate. "Really though, did you really think you were going to get away with that?"

Maybe Samantha was right about my moral compass being broken.

"I don't get it," I protested. "What's with you? Do you want me to lie and cheat, or not lie and cheat? What do you want?"

"What do *you* want, Higgs? Really, what do you want? College? Harvard? That whole entitlement thing?"

"You think I'm a jerk just because I'm going to Harvard. Wait. Correction. Might go to Harvard."

"I think you're a bourgeoisie jerk for even wanting to go there in the first place. Do you know what kind of people go to places like that?" Monarch didn't wait for my answer. "Rich people who don't give a shit about others. Rich people who live off of their daddy's money, and live in a bubble, and are too scared to stand up for themselves."

Clearly this was a sore point for her.

"Did you take an SAT class?" she asked.

I nodded.

"Did you have a college admissions coach?"

I nodded.

"Did you apply to multiple colleges?"

I nodded.

"Did you retake your SAT to bring your average up?"

I nodded.

"Did your parents pull strings to help you?"

I nodded.

"Well?" she said.

"Well now you've made me feel like shit," I said. I looked out the window at the streetlights rushing past.

"Some people really have to struggle to get into college," she said. "Others are handed everything even though they don't deserve it, or even want it."

For a moment, she looked sad. I wondered if she was one of those people who wanted to go to college.

Monarch shook off her melancholy and replaced it with a wicked smile. "Now, Higgs, if you are truly repentant, you must atone for your sins."

"How?"

I could see the silhouette of the water tower looming as Rolvo slowed. "You must rescue real animals in need," she advised, sounding very priestly.

I wasn't Catholic, but I went to mass with Nick a lot when we were younger. I always asked God for the same thing . . . to make my parents happy.

"I'm serious," she said. "If you want to stay my friend, you have to rescue animals, real animals who are in jeopardy. You *do* want to stay my friend, don't you, Higgs?"

I nodded.

Monarch let out a whoop that was louder than any cowboy's. "This is going to be so great. I've always wanted to rescue animals!"

As Monarch babbled, I turned on my phone. There were twelve text messages. Most were from my father.

Harvard admin phone interview Sat @ 4
My lawyer ready to prep you.
Answer me!

There was a text from Mom. Honey, are you okay? Love u.

And one from Charlie. Mom's a wreck. Dad's a douche. U r in trouble.

I turned my phone off.

"Bing! Let's go rescue animals!" Monarch said gleefully.

What had I gotten myself into? When I considered my options — going home to Mom melting down and Dad angry — suddenly, rescuing animals seemed like fun.

"Sure," I told her. "But not today, tomorrow."

Monarch looked deflated. "You're chickening out on me, aren't you?"

"No," I swore. "Really, I want to do this." And the odd thing was, I did. "But I need to go home. I want to check on my mom."

Monarch nodded. "Okay, but remember, you promised to do a rescue."

A rescue. If only I could rescue my parents' marriage. My college fiasco. Monarch. Myself.

Day 4

CHAPTER 30

Dad was gone. The house was quiet except for some excessively cheerful lady on the television extolling the virtues of a self-cleaning damp mop. I picked up the remote and hit "off."

Mom's door was closed. I pressed my ear against it, but all I heard was silence. There was a thin slice of light coming out from under Charlie's door. I knocked softly.

"Go away," she said. Her voice sounded muffled.

Even though it was dark, I went out to my garden. I flipped the switch and the floodlights lit up the backyard — day for night. The tomatoes had ripened, threatening to snap the vines. The deep dark green zucchini looked good and so did the yellow squash. The Bing cherries were shiny, ripe, and red — perfect. How could they not be? I made sure to pick plenty, and a few peaches too. In my small plot of land, I had managed to grow a whole produce section.

I worked for what seemed like hours. Cleaning out the weeds.

Picking the ripe fruit and vegetables. Staking the tomatoes. Watering.

I brought my bounty into the house and washed and polished each apple, each zucchini, everything, individually. Then I got out the paper bags, and when they were full, I left them at the doors of some of our neighbors. I didn't need to leave a note, they'd know who it was from. When I was done, I had one bag left.

Thursday

Day 3

CHAPTER 31

I woke up to the smell of bacon frying. When I went into Charlie's room, her bed was empty. The sheets were strewn around and Bunchy Bear was trapped between the mattress and the wall. I rescued him and set him on top of Charlie's pillow. Even after all these years, he still smelled like Jeffrey, kind of like the woods and soap.

Mom was at the stove flipping pancakes, something she hadn't done in years. Usually we ate cereal. My sister was already seated. Dad's chair was noticeably empty. When Jeffrey was alive, breakfast was a big deal at our house. Sometimes he'd cook bacon, eggs, the works, even though everyone was always in a hurry to leave. It was choreographed chaos with Jeffrey as the ringleader. Unlike the rest of us, my brother was a morning person. He'd have some music blasting on the radio, and would hand cups of coffee to Mom and Dad as they straggled into the kitchen. And even though everyone was grumpy, he'd tell jokes and tease us until we were all smiling.

"Why didn't you wake me up?" I asked as I poured myself a glass of milk.

"You're a big boy, you can wake yourself up," Charlie said. "Besides, I'm not going to Harvard with you, so you're going to have to practice getting up on your own."

My mother and I glanced at each other.

"What?" Charlie said defensively. "I saw that. Is this about me?"

"It's about me," I said.

"It's always about you," she muttered as she drizzled loops of maple syrup over her pancakes.

"Hey, Mom, how are you doing?" I asked.

"Just fine, Higgs," my mother said, smiling. She put a stack of perfect pancakes on my plate, then kissed me on the top of the head.

The odd thing was, she looked like she was fine. Mom's hair was pulled back and she was wearing her favorite dress, the plain one with the daisies on it. Unlike Dad with his Porsche and fancy suits, my mother had never been flashy. It was such a joy to see her without the Robe of Depression.

"I'm getting vibes that there's something someone's not telling me," my sister said through a mouthful of pancake. "What's the big secret, Dinky?"

"Charlie!" my mother scolded.

"It's okay, Mom," I said. I took a swig of milk. "Remember that movie Nick and I made about rescuing his dog?"

Charlie faked a yawn. "Yeah, they forced us to watch it at assembly."

"Well, Harvard is questioning the authenticity of the Society for Animal Protection."

My sister's eyes widened. "Higgs . . . are they going to kick you out?"

"That remains to be seen," I said. "I . . . I . . . I have to talk to someone from Admissions Review."

"You'll do fine," my mother assured me. "Just be yourself, Higgs, and you'll have nothing to worry about."

But that was the problem. I hadn't been myself for years.

The doorbell rang and we all looked up. Maybe it was my father, and he had forgotten his key. Maybe he was coming home to beg Mom for forgiveness. But it was neither. It was just Mrs. Pincus, stopping by to thank me for the vegetables.

As I was about to shut the door, a black Porsche with Harvard plates pulled into the driveway. Before my father could even get out of the car, I was in his face.

"Why? Can you tell me why?"

He shook his head slowly. There were bags under his eyes, and he hadn't shaved. His shoulders slumped. He looked like shit. "I don't know" was all he said. "I just came back to get some of my things. Help me, won't you, Higgs?"

There was a chill in the air when my father greeted my mom and Charlie. As they both stiffened, I could see Dad deflate. The painless dentist was in pain.

My father had brought boxes and began to haphazardly throw his clothes into them. He didn't even bother to close the dresser drawers when he was done. My parents' room looked like a tornado had blown through it. He left the mess for my mother to clean up.

"Bring these to the car, won't you, Higgs?" he said. "I've got to get stuff from the den."

"Maybe you could just say you were wrong and beg for forgiveness," I suggested.

He gave me a sad smile and said, "I think it may be too late for that."

As I took the first box, I noticed something pink on the floor. I grabbed the Robe of Depression and tossed it into Rolvo on my way to my father's car. My mother would never think of looking there for it.

As usual, Dad's Porsche was spotless. Maybe if he paid more attention to his wife than his car, they wouldn't be splitting up. I set the box on the front seat. A couple of shirts fell on the floor, and when I picked them up, I noticed something tucked under the passenger seat. It was a small black velvet box. There was a lump in my throat. Inside was a necklace with an "M" set in diamonds. My mother never wore stuff like that. She had always made it very clear that she thought expensive jewelry was a waste of money. Plus, her name was Elizabeth.

I slipped the necklace into my pocket.

Day 3

CHAPTER 32

I put Monarch's produce in the backseat, next to the Robe of Depression, then took the velvet box out of my pocket. The necklace was excessive. The kind of gift you'd give someone you were trying to impress. I wondered when my parents stopped trying to impress each other. Charlie slid into the passenger seat, and I quickly closed the box and tossed it into the backseat so she wouldn't ask any questions.

"This is our last morning driving to school together," Charlie announced.

It was Thursday. Seniors didn't have to go to school on Friday.

I turned the engine on. "Yep."

"Listen, Higgs," Charlie said, getting serious. "You have to go to Harvard."

Her concern touched me.

"Because, if you don't," she continued, "you'll still be here and I won't get Rolvo."

"I love you too, Charlie," I said.

"How did it feel when everyone called you Dinky Dick?" she asked.

"What do you think?" I said. "It felt awful."

"Any idea who did the flyers and stuff?"

"I thought I did at first. But now I'm not really sure."

"What'll you do when you figure it out?"

I shook my head. "I don't know, Charlie. Kill them?"

The novelty of calling me a Dinky Dick seemed to have worn off. Most kids seemed to have other things on their minds that morning. The majority were giddy, a few looked sad. Zander Findley was talking to Roo. Both pretended not to see me. Princeton could have him. Saturday, I would tackle Harvard. Maybe I could talk my way out of my dilemma — I'd always been a good talker. Wait. That wasn't true.

"Hey, Higgs!" Zander said as Roo took off.

My jaw automatically clenched. "What do you want?" I asked. "Besides my girlfriend."

"She's not your girlfriend anymore," he said, taking pleasure in reminding me. I crossed my arms and waited to hear what he had to say next. "Can you believe Lauren Fujiyama?" he asked. "I mean, seriously?"

I knew what he meant. She was a long shot for Senior of the Year. Anyone could have predicted me winning, or even Zander. But Lauren?

"Did you do it?" I asked.

"Do what?"

"You know."

"Listen, I would love to take credit for Dinky Dick," Zander said, "but it wasn't me. That's not my style. I would have called you a douche, or an asshole, or a cretin. But 'Dinky Dick'? No."

"What about Harvard?" I asked.

"What about Harvard?" he asked.

"You really don't know?"

He shook his head, and when I told him, Zander Findley was speechless.

"I hate you, Higgs," he finally said. "But I would never do something like that. Shit. Do you think they're going to come after more people? God, I hope not. My parents paid a journalist to edit my personal essay. Everyone cheats. Everyone."

"Yeah, well I'm the only one being called on it," I said bitterly.

"That sucks," he said.

For once, Zander Findley and I were in agreement.

We watched the kids buzzing around us. Mr. French was picking up trash over by the cafeteria.

"Are you going to miss high school?" I asked him.

"Parts of it," he said. "But Princeton, that's where I belong. My parents met there. So, what are you going to do about Harvard? Can you go somewhere else if they don't take you?"

"It's too late, I'd have to wait a semester and then reapply to another college. Anyway, there's still a good chance they'll let me in. I just have to convince them of my innocence."

"You're a great bullshitter," Zander conceded.

"Same to you," I replied, returning the compliment.

Zander Findley wasn't so bad. Sure, he was smart, and arrogant, and competitive. In other words, he was just like me. Maybe that's why I hated him so much.

The morning was spent in our final rehearsal for graduation. Even though it was blazing hot on the football field, we all had to practice lining up and marching in — this time in our caps and gowns. Lots of kids wore their gowns backward and carried their caps just to piss Mr. Avis off. No one was taking rehearsal seriously.

Zander, Lauren, and I sat on the stage and were supposed to rehearse our speeches. I knew that Zander would probably say something about overcoming challenges, and that Lauren would probably get all mushy and thank the parents. My speech was your basic "As I stand before you today, I reflect on the morning I started high school, a short four years ago. In that time, I have learned . . . blah, blah, blah." It was all bullshit. Everything was bullshit. My parents' marriage. My reputation. Graduation. My Harvard application. Bullshit. Bullshit. Bullshit.

As Mr. Avis was unsuccessfully trying to get the class's attention, I stood up.

"Mr. Bing, where do you think you are going?" he asked.

"Anywhere but here," I told him as I continued walking. Suddenly, all eyes were on us.

"Do not take one more step," Mr. Avis ordered.

I turned to face him.

"You step off that stage and we will only have two senior commencement speakers on Saturday."

I took another step.

"Mr. Bing, did you hear me?" Mr. Avis demanded into the microphone.

Everyone heard him. The football field was silent. I could see Nick with his mouth hanging open. Samantha Verve gave me the finger. Roo blinked and stared blankly at me, like she didn't know who I was.

No one moved.

No one but me.

Day 3

CHAPTER 33

I had just walked my way out of a commencement speech that for years I had visualized myself giving. The last time we had graduation practice, everyone was laughing at me. This time, they were cheering. No one called me Dinky Dick when I stood up to Mr. Avis. For the first time in a long time, I felt free. Except for graduation, I was done with high school, forever.

I had never been truant before, but what could they do to me now? Besides, I had promised Monarch that I was going to do an animal rescue.

I sprinted across the gravel pit, carrying the bag of fruit and vegetables from my garden. Monarch wasn't in her trailer, so I let myself in. I filled a battered pot with Bing cherries, then took out the tomatoes and placed them on a plate. I wished I had brought a loaf of French bread. There was no place to store the rest of the produce, so I left it in the bag and waited.

A navy-blue backpack was tucked in the corner, under some newspapers. I looked out the dusty windows. With no Monarch in sight, and my curiosity getting the better of me, I unzipped the backpack. There was a jar of hard candies, several composition books, and a couple of fountain pens. I opened one of the books. Inside were sketches — bridges, old buildings, the Eiffel Tower . . .

"HIGGS!"

Startled, I dropped the notebook.

"I . . . you . . . I thought."

Monarch's eyes flashed. She grabbed the book off the floor before I could hand it to her.

"I'm sorry," I began.

She wouldn't let me finish.

"I can't believe you would go through my personal private things," she said, managing to sound mortally wounded and like she was going to kill me at the same time.

"I brought you a present," I mumbled, reaching for a tomato and holding it out to her. "I grew it myself."

Monarch eyed the tomato and the cherries in the pot. I handed her the bag with the rest of the fruit and vegetables in it. "These are for you," I said in a rush. "Everything. I picked them especially for you."

Still angry, she took the bag. "You really think a bag of vegetables can make up for invading my privacy?" She held up a zucchini. "Oh, look. This ought to equalize the fact that you were snooping." Suddenly, Monarch's voice broke. "What did you do, Higgs? What's this?"

"I grew everything myself," I repeated. "I've got almost a quarter acre of my own at home, and I've been growing things since, well, since I was a little kid."

Monarch shook her head. "This is what I was asking about," she said, holding something up. Her voice went soft. "Higgs, is this for me?"

In her hand was a black velvet box. Damn, I must have tossed it into the bag. Words caught in my throat, and when I didn't answer, she opened it. Her eyes grew huge. "Oh my god! Is this for real? It can't be real!"

Before I could even explain that my father had bought it for his girlfriend or his mistress or his whatever, Monarch was putting the diamond necklace on.

"Higgs," she murmured. "Oh, Higgs." She fished around her purse for a compact mirror and admired herself. That Monarch would be so thrilled with jewelry surprised me. "It's beautiful. A diamond 'M.' Seriously, no one's ever given me jewelry like this before. Thank you."

When Monarch kissed me on the cheek, I could feel my face burn red.

I took a deep breath. Suddenly, my tomatoes and cherries seemed insignificant.

Day 3

CHAPTER 34

Petty's Pets was located at the far end of the Monte Vista Mall. I used to always beg my mother to take me there when I was little. Every time we'd go, I'd head straight to the hamster cages. I was mesmerized by the furry rodents running circles inside their exercise wheels. They always seemed to be in a hurry, but for what, I could never figure out.

The last time I had been to Petty's Pets was with Jeffrey. He took me there the day before he was leaving for college. It was exciting spending time with him, just the two of us. Yet it made me sad too. That he was going away.

That morning, Jeffrey had made breakfast for everyone. But Dad was in a hurry and just grabbed a piece of toast. Mom was on a diet, and didn't touch her eggs Benedict. Charlie was little and refused to eat anything other than Froot Loops. So, not only did I eat my entire breakfast, I tried to eat everyone else's too, hoping that Jeffrey wouldn't feel bad.

I worshipped my big brother and would do anything for him. He was everything I was not — popular, handsome, smart, athletic. I was just your average forgettable skinny fourth grader with a debilitating stutter.

Jeffrey had heard that Petty's Pets had put in a reptile section and wanted to see the snakes. Near the entrance, huge waterless aquariums were filled with dirt and rocks, and branches. They looked empty. But Jeffrey showed me how you had to look carefully since the snakes blended in so well in the fake desert that they were practically invisible. "Things aren't always as they first appear," he told me.

Just as we were about to leave, one of the Petty's Pets clerks opened a nearby cage of mice. I thought that maybe someone was going to buy one, they looked so small and cute. The clerk reached in and grabbed a random mouse. I tugged on Jeffrey's shirt. "He looks like Stuart Little," I said, pointing. My mother was in the middle of reading that book to me and Charlie. I liked that Stuart could drive a car.

Jeffrey started to say something but stopped when we saw the clerk lift the top of the snake aquarium and dangle the mouse over it.

"Dinnertime!" the man announced before dropping the terrified mouse into the aquarium.

Out of nowhere, a slender orange snake appeared. The mouse froze, and so did I. Then, in one lightning-quick move, the snake struck. I remember trying to scream, but no sound came out. To this day, I still sometimes wake up in a cold sweat, dreaming about the outline of the mouse's body inside the snake.

*   *   *

"What are we doing at the mall?" Monarch asked as she parked Rolvo across two parking spaces. She adjusted the mirror to admire the necklace again. "I thought you were supposed to be rescuing animals, not shopping."

"Just follow me," I told her.

Petty's Pets was still there. The familiar smell of wood shavings, and urine, and damp animals hit me on the way in. As Monarch cooed at the puppies in the front of the store, I scoped out the place. The hamsters and the fish were in the same location, but the reptiles had been moved to the back. Nearby was a cage full of white mice. A handwritten sign read "For pets or pet food."

"No way!" Monarch said from behind me. She leaned down and peered into the cage. "They can't be serious!"

"Here's the plan," I said, lowering my voice.

Monarch started laughing so hard that several people stared at her. "Oh, Higgs," she said, trying to compose herself. "If we pull this off, you're going to be my hero."

I warmed at the thought of it.

As planned, we waited until more people were in the store. There were only three clerks. Two girls gabbing at the register, and one guy roaming the aisles.

"Excuse me, sir," Monarch said to the clerk. He was wearing a "Petty's Pets Expert Ricky" name tag. "Do you know where I could buy a bear cub?"

"Uh, no," Ricky said. He had a buzz cut and the unsatisfactory beginnings of a beard.

"Hmmm, all right. Then what about monkeys? A friend of mine has a pet monkey, and I want one too so they can have playdates."

Ricky shook his head, "No, no monkeys," he told her as he adjusted his collar. It was tight on his thick neck.

"Okay, then what about turtles?" Monarch asked, taking a step toward him. "Ricky, please tell me you have turtles."

A slow smile crossed Ricky's broad face. "Turtles we have," he said triumphantly. "Follow me."

As Monarch went to look at the turtles, I went to look at the mice. The aisle was empty. The mice were so packed into the wire cage that they were climbing over one another. Carefully, I propped the door open. A little girl wearing a crown and holding a lollipop was watching me.

"Go away," I hissed.

She shook her head.

"Get out of here."

She still refused to move and didn't until I growled at her.

From across the store, I could see Monarch and Ricky. She was asking, "Ferrets? Do you have ferrets? What country are they from?"

I pushed the cage to the edge of the counter so that it was hanging precariously over the ledge.

"You don't have sharks?" I could hear her ask. "No? Well, what about snakes? Do you have snakes?"

As Ricky led Monarch to the snakes, I retreated. She looked into one of the aquariums and said, "Ricky, I know you're teasing me, there's no snake in there."

He smiled at Monarch. "No, I swear, there's one in there, you just have to look carefully."

"I don't believe you," she said coyly. "Show me."

Ricky removed the lid from the aquarium, reached in, and pulled out a corn snake. When he triumphantly held it out, Monarch released an impressive scream before backing into the open cage of mice and knocking them onto the floor. Ricky lurched toward the cage, dropping the snake, which immediately slithered after a mouse.

"Save me!" Monarch screamed, throwing her arms around him.

As the mice scampered around the store, chaos ensued and it was glorious. Holding hands, Monarch and I moved toward the door. That's when I noticed a mouse, huddled up against a display. "You can go," I told him. "Get out of here, you're free!"

The mouse was paralyzed with fear.

"We'd better leave," Monarch whispered above the screaming customers. "Ricky's giving me a funny look."

I scooped up the mouse and slipped him into my pocket.

Day 3

CHAPTER 35

Monarch and I were in the parking lot, laughing and congratulating ourselves.

"So, am I your hero?" I asked.

"Higgs Boson Bing, you are *so* my hero!" she exclaimed.

We stared at each other, and in a romantic-movie moment, I brushed some hair out of her eyes and took a step toward her. I was about to kiss Monarch when she broke the spell by asking awkwardly, "So, what's his or her name?"

I was almost surprised to find myself holding a mouse. It was quivering in the palm of my hand and looked scared.

"Stuart," I said without hesitation. I straightened up, as if kissing her had never been part of the plan.

"Stuart?" Monarch said, scrunching up her nose. "I was thinking of Annabelle —" She stopped and motioned toward the mall. Ricky was coming toward us with a grim look plastered on his face. Behind him was a heavy mall security guard speaking into a walkie-talkie.

"Get in the car," I told Monarch. "Hurry, before they catch us!"

Monarch climbed into the driver's side and fumbled to get the keys in the ignition.

"Put it in gear! Put it in gear!" I shouted as Ricky and the mall cop began sprinting. "Goddamn it, put the car in gear!!!"

"Don't yell at me!" Monarch screamed, near tears. "I'm trying."

"Put it in gear," I shouted.

She pumped the pedal but we didn't move.

"Holy crap, put it in gear!" I was well aware that my screaming had reached new levels of shrill, but I couldn't control it any more than I could control Monarch.

She let out a yelp as the out-of-breath mall cop lumbered straight toward us and began pounding Rolvo's hood. I couldn't hear what he was yelling, but Ricky kept pointing and waving his arms. My adrenaline was in overdrive even though my car was not.

"Put it in gear," I shouted once more.

"Oh, in gear," Monarch purred. "Higgs, why didn't you say so?"

Like a female James Bond, Monarch threw Rolvo into gear and did a couple laps around Ricky and the mall cop before peeling out of the parking lot.

Just as we were about to make a clean getaway, Monarch yanked on the emergency break and Rolvo did a 180. Then Monarch rolled up to the red-faced Ricky, who looked stunned. I doubt anyone had ever seen a Volvo station wagon perform like that.

"Ricky, dear Ricky," Monarch said, pouting. "Now, who am I going to go to when I need a penguin?"

Before Ricky could even begin to process what was happening, Monarch let go of one of her cowboy hoots and away we went.

I wasn't sure what just happened, but I was convinced that we were in trouble. As we sped onto the freeway, I gripped the seat with one hand and held Stuart with the other. Fear and panic were tinged with elation. I had never felt so free.

"That was fun, wasn't it?" Monarch said.

"No," I said, my voice sounding higher pitched than usual. Trying to breathe normally was difficult. "I don't know why you went back to make fun of Ricky. Now they've gotten a good look at us. We could have gotten arrested."

Monarch let go of a long laugh. "Seriously? By a mall cop? I don't think so. Calm down, Ivy League. We're just having kicks, okay?"

She patted my thigh.

"So then," Monarch continued. "Tell me why our rescue mouse is named Stuart. Is there some sort of cultural or sociological significance to that?"

"My mother read *Stuart Little* to me," I explained. "I loved it so much that when she reached the last page, I made her start over again immediately. When I was little I felt like him, like an oddity."

"Why?"

"Because I stuttered and wasn't good at much. My big brother, Jeffrey, was the king and my father had little time for anyone else. When Dad did pay attention to me, I'd get so overwhelmed, my stutter would get worse."

"Did he get mad at you for that?" Monarch asked.

"He never said anything, but my father couldn't look at me when I was sputtering and stammering."

The memory of those days caused a sharp pain to shoot through me.

"You certainly don't have any trouble speaking now," Monarch said. "So what's Jeffrey up to these days? Still king of the world?"

"We buried him on the day I turned nine, not that anyone noticed it was my birthday —"

"Higgs . . . I am so sorry." She sounded sincere.

I looked in the side mirror. There was a police car following us. I checked the speedometer. When the car pulled alongside us, my body went rigid as I stared straight ahead. This was a real cop, not a mall cop.

"Do not speed. Do not swerve. Do not swear. Do not do anything," I whispered to Monarch even though the cop couldn't hear me.

For once, Monarch did what she was told.

After what seemed like an hour, but probably was only a couple of minutes or less, the police car pulled in front of us and took off.

I slumped back into my seat and held my head in my hands. "Oh my god!" I screamed. "I can't believe this."

"Are you going to be all right?" Monarch asked.

I nodded. "Yeah, I thought we were going to get pulled over."

"We did nothing wrong," she said.

"Not according to Ricky and Petty's Pets," I reminded her.

"That was nothing," Monarch said, brushing it aside. "Hey, Higgs. You were talking about your dad and your brother. What you said was pretty intense."

"Oh, that. Whatever," I said, shrugging. "Forget I even mentioned it."

I know I was trying to.

Day 3

CHAPTER 36

We were parked outside the iffy Mart. Night had fallen. Monarch had a fresh pack of cigarettes and I was in possession of a large cherry slush bomb and a Mr. Gooey Chewy. I hadn't had one in years. My father hated all candy, especially ones that could pull out your teeth.

The Mr. Gooey Chewy tasted like Christmas. As I chewed and chewed and chewed, I took out a package of unnaturally bright orange cheese and tore a corner off for Stuart. He seemed cautious at first, then began to nibble. I liked watching him eat. I gave him more.

Monarch and I were sitting on Rolvo's hood, something I had never done in my entire life. The silver BMW was on the other side of the lot, and so were two blue Mini Coopers, parked side by side. "Do you think they'll find us?" I asked. "I wonder what would happen if we got caught."

Monarch traced the rooster on her lighter with her finger, then lit up her second cigarette. "No one's gonna catch us," she assured me as she blew smoke out of the side of her mouth. "We're smarter than pet store people."

"How can you be so sure?"

"I just am," she said confidently. "So then, let's talk about Higgs Boson Bing." I hoped she didn't want to continue our conversation about Jeffrey, so I was relieved when Monarch asked, "Who hates you?"

"What kind of a question is that?"

I fished a shoe box out of the dumpster and lined the bottom with newspaper before gently setting Stuart inside.

"It's a perfectly good question," Monarch answered as she watched me use a pen to poke holes in the lid of the box. "I'm going to help you figure out who's trying to bring you down. C'mon, fess up, Higgs. There must be lots of people who want to see you fall."

"Golly, gee. Thanks, Monarch."

"Oh, there you go again, getting your feelings hurt. Of course people hate you, Higgs."

"Why would you say something like that? Why?"

"You really want to know?"

Against my better judgment, I nodded.

"Well, first of all, you've got that good-looking thing going for you."

I tried not to smile when I heard that. Maybe Monarch's assessment of me wouldn't be too painful after all.

Then she continued. "You reek of good breeding. Well spoken to a fault. And you're smug. Plus, there's the sense of entitlement. And cheating on your Harvard application?" Monarch shook her head. "That's low. If someone went to all the effort of making those flyers, they must hate you."

I had heard enough.

"Do you hate me?" I asked.

"Is that your bonus question?"

I shook my head. I was fairly certain Monarch didn't hate me. Why else would she have spent all that time with me? Was it the money? I wondered. I bought groceries for her, let her drive Rolvo. Hell, I gave her a diamond necklace.

Monarch continued puffing on her cigarette, acting oblivious to me sitting next to her. She had a small scar on her chin.

"Stop it, Higgs."

"Stop what?"

"Stop staring at me like that, it's creepy."

"What about you?" I asked.

"What about me?"

"What's your story? How come you get to ask me questions, but I'm limited to what I can ask you? Where is the justice in that?"

"There is no justice in this world. So tell me, who hates you?" she said, stubbing out her cigarette. "I want to crack this case."

I took another bite of my candy bar and was glad that it took me so long to chew it. Then I began.

Day 3

CHAPTER 37

As I went through my suspect list, Monarch listened carefully. "... I was pretty sure it was Rosalee Gomez."

"Why would she do something like that?"

"Because we made out," I said.

Monarch whistled. "Wow, you're that bad, huh?"

I had to laugh. "No, I'm actually really good. Would you like to find out for yourself?"

"In your dreams."

"Anyway, she wanted us to be more than we were. A woman scorned and all that."

"Okay, next. Tell me more about Mr. Hertz."

"Avis," I corrected her. "It's Mr. Avis. ..."

"You tried to get your assistant principal fired?" Monarch asked after I told her about him. I thought I detected a hint of admiration in her voice.

Stuart crawled up and down my arm. "There were lots of others involved, but he's always had it out for me."

"Okay. Who's next?"

I told her about Samantha Verve, and how Zander Findley and I have never liked each other.

"What did you do to him?"

"I don't even know. Or maybe he did something to me. We've been enemies for as long as I can remember. Neither of us has ever talked about it. We both just hate each other. But he seemed genuinely surprised when I told him about the Harvard thing."

"Give me another name."

"For a while, I thought it might be Mr. French, the school janitor. He's the definition of a dick. Drives a car that's so old the windows won't even roll up. I'll bet he sleeps in that thing.

"There's nothing wrong with not having a house," I hastened to add. I had forgotten that Monarch lived in the woods. "But you should see this guy, he's just a loser. He's like forty and still working as a janitor at the very same school he graduated from. Or maybe he didn't even graduate —" I could hear myself digging my grave even deeper. Chances were that Monarch didn't graduate from high school. I wondered how long, if ever, she even went. Still, she was pretty well read. But then, Albert Einstein didn't graduate from high school. Not that Monarch was Albert Einstein.

"Hey, then there's Roo," I offered up, in hopes that we could change the subject. "She was my girlfriend for over two years."

Monarch sparked to the word "girlfriend." She sat up and looked interested. "Did you love her?"

I shook my head. "No, we were just . . . together, that's all."

"Did she love you?"

I let go of a deep sigh. "Well, she told me she did about twenty times a day."

"How did you feel about that?"

"At first, it was disconcerting, then it was nice, but after a while, it was just annoying. Every time she said it, I could tell she was waiting for me to say 'I love you' back."

"So did you say it?"

"Sometimes, but it's not the sort of thing you should say if you're not really sure. Right? I mean if you're going to say it, then it should be the real thing."

Monarch gave me a wicked smile. "My, my, Higgs Boson Bing is a romantic?"

"Hell no!" I said, setting her straight. "Romance is overrated."

"So what caused the split?"

"A hypothetical about whether I'd give her one of my kidneys."

"I hate hypotheticals," Monarch said.

My heart soared when I heard this.

"Is there anyone else on your list?"

I nodded. "Nick," I told her. "He's my best friend."

"Tell me about Nick."

"Nick Milgram and I have been best friends practically all our lives," I began slowly. I struggled to find my voice. "We met in second grade. He was the new kid, but neither of us had any friends."

"Why?"

"I was small, and I talked funny. You know, stuttering and stammering."

Monarch didn't say anything. Her silence reminded me of Dr. Raleigh's. She didn't say much either.

I took a deep breath. "My parents were busy building their separate universes. Mom worked for the Jet Propulsion Lab in robotics. She was on the Cassini mission and a real rising star. Dad's practice was taking off too. He was getting a lot of attention, mainly because of his 'painless dentist' ads."

"I don't like dentists," Monarch said. I tried not to take it personally. "Dentists and doctors and lawyers," she continued. "They are all so pretentious. Scientists are okay."

"Mom was always working late, or on the road, speaking at science conferences and stuff. Dad was doing his own thing, so that left me and my brother, Jeffrey, at home all the time, and then later, with Charlie, my sister."

"Alone?" Monarch asked.

I shook my head. "No, we had a nanny, Marie."

I checked on Stuart. He looked up at me with his little red eyes and wiggled his nose. I gave him some more cheese. He had me trained well.

"I was always following Jeffrey around. He was ten years older, but I think he took pity on me. I pretty much clung to him, until I met Nick.

"At school, lots of kids used to tease me about the way I talked. But not Nick. He never made fun of me and I never made fun of him either. Back in those days, he wasn't book smart like he is now. In second grade, he couldn't even read. So there we were, two losers. One who couldn't read and one who couldn't talk."

Monarch took the Mr. Gooey Chewy from me, took a bite, and gave it back. "So how did Nick learn how to read?" she asked.

I broke into a big grin. "I taught him. I'd read to him, but I had to go slow because of my stutter. Yet slow was exactly what

174

he needed. And ironically, the repetition of the stuttering helped. Well, that and the reading teacher his parents hired. But I like to think that it was mostly me. I also started going to a speech therapist at school. Zander Findley was there too. His stutter was worse than mine, though I'm sure he'd deny that. It's something we've never discussed."

I laughed at the thought of it. Higgs Boson Bing and Zander Findley, Sally Ride High School's top two leaders, started out as losers in speech therapy. I knew who he used to be, and he knew who I was. It would have been double suicide if either one of us revealed the truth about the other.

"Go on," Monarch urged.

I cupped my hands around Stuart. "Jeffrey excelled in everything he did. My parents were so proud of him. 'He's my Harvard legacy,' Dad used to boast. 'The next generation of Bing dentist!' My father was big on this legacy thing. Mom had always wanted a girl, so she doted on Charlie, her little princess — and then there was me. Stuttering Higgs. Mediocre grades. Medium height. Nothing special. If it weren't for Nick, elementary school would have been hell. But it wasn't. We had fun. I never stuttered around Nick.

"After he began to read, teachers discovered what I knew all along. That Nick was really smart. And he knew all along that I had things to say. We'd pretend to be Batman and Robin. Only, we took turns being Batman since neither one of us wanted to be the sidekick.

"So one day I came home from Nick's. It was a Friday afternoon. Mom's and Dad's cars were in the driveway, which was weird, because they were hardly ever home during the day. Marie met me at the door. Her eyes were red. She was cradling Charlie, who would have been five. Marie started to say something — and that's when I heard it. It was the most awful noise. It didn't sound human, but it was. It was my mother."

Monarch didn't say anything, but by the way her lips were pursed, I could tell she was worried. The ash on her cigarette grew long. I got off of Rolvo and started pacing. It felt like my organs were collapsing.

"Higgs?"

I started to cry. Silently, at first, then full-out sobbing, making sounds like I heard that day coming from my mother. Monarch didn't move, and I almost forgot she was there. I was hysterical and she had the grace not to mention it.

I placed Stuart gently in the box and secured the lid. "I don't want him to drown," I tried to joke.

"We don't have to talk about this," Monarch said softly.

"It's okay." I took big greedy gulps of air. "I want to."

I jumped up and down a few times, to shake off my stress, and then explained, "My brother died in a car crash. He was drunk and slammed his Corolla into a light post. I stopped talking completely. My parents were so worried about me they sent me to a therapist. Dr. Raleigh tried to get me to open up. Twice a week, Tuesday and Thursday, fifty-five minutes per session. It was pretty much a waste of my parents' money since I had nothing to say. But somehow that made them feel better.

"Mom quit her job to be home with Charlie and me. Dad really dove into his job even more.

" 'Higgs, are you all right?' my mother would ask.

" 'Higgs, don't do this,' my father would say.

"'Higgs, are you there?' Charlie would ask, peering into my eyes.

"The only person who didn't question me was Nick. Sometimes he'd read Batman comics to me. Other times, we just hung around. We didn't need to talk. When I wasn't with Nick, I was in the garden. Mom started the garden on the recommendation of her therapist. It was something we did together.

"Then one day, I saw something I wasn't supposed to —"

I shut my eyes tight at the memory of it.

Monarch leaned in toward me. "What did you see, Higgs?"

I shook my head, but I could still see it.

"It was nighttime," I continued, "and, as always, my father was late coming home. My mother had given me some asparagus to take to our neighbors on the next block. We grew so much we were always giving stuff away. I liked doing that. I still do.

"Anyway, on my way to the neighbors', I saw my father's Porsche parked around the corner. I started running toward it, but stopped before he saw me. Dad was just sitting in his car, crying. I had never seen him cry before. That's all my mother did. But my father was stoic, even at the funeral. Thanking people for coming. Shaking their hands. Comforting them as my mother stood by his side and sobbed. All the while, Charlie and I leaned against each other with our heads down, allowing ourselves to be hugged by strangers.

"When I saw my father, I was shaken. He wasn't just weeping — no, he was really crying and yelling, and he was slamming his fist on the dashboard. I had never been so scared in my life. That's when I decided that I'd do anything to make him stop. To make him feel better."

"So what did you do?" Monarch asked, her eyes wide. "What could you do? You were just a kid."

"I knocked on the car door and my father looked up, surprised. He wiped his tears and I got in and sat in the passenger seat. We were both silent for the longest time, and then I asked, 'Are you going to be all right?' No stutter, no stammer.

"My father looked surprised. 'Yes, Higgs,' he said. 'Thank you for asking.' Then he hugged me and told me he loved me. He had never said that before.

"At that moment, it was like I had channeled Jeffrey. I decided that I would be my father's Harvard legacy. I would be all that Jeffrey couldn't be —"

Before I could finish, we were interrupted by a scratching noise. I took Stuart out of the box and handed him to Monarch while I went into the iffy Mart and returned with a bottle of water. I filled the cap and set it on Rolvo's hood. Wordlessly, Monarch handed me my mouse.

I offered Stuart some more cheese, but he declined, instead preferring to run up and down my arm a bit. After a while, he slowed down, nestled into the palm of my hand, and went to sleep. He looked so peaceful.

"Let me hold him," she said, cradling him in her hands.

Just then the revving of an engine startled Stuart awake. I looked up to see a pickup truck with flames painted on it rolling to a stop, boxing Rolvo into the parking space.

"Look at that," I said to Monarch. "Seriously?"

"What's the matter, can't you read?" the passenger yelled.

A "Reserved for Mixxed Martial Arts AAcademy" sign was in front of Rolvo. Had it always been there?

"There are plenty of other spaces," I yelled back.

"Move your damn truck," Monarch yelled. "We were here first!"

"Well, well," a man said as he got out of the passenger side. He was wearing a too-tight WWE tank top that showed off his muscles. Steroids? He had a tattoo of a bodybuilder on his bicep, which seemed redundant. "Watch your mouth, darling," he said to Monarch.

"Fuck off," she said. Monarch took a deep draw on her cigarette, then tossed it in his direction.

"Don't piss him off," I whispered under my breath.

The bodybuilder looked Monarch up and down, then winked. "Do you belong to that kid?" he asked, motioning to me. " 'Cause darling, you don't need a boy, you need a man."

Monarch scoffed. "Well, if you ever meet a man, be sure to let me know," she said.

Out of nowhere, a double-edged knife was in his hand. "You're pretty sassy," he said, holding the blade under her chin. She didn't move, but her eyes flickered before going blank.

I was frozen.

"What's the matter? Cat got your tongue?" he said, looking at Monarch like he wanted to eat her up. He licked his lips.

She pushed his knife away. "Don't point that or anything else you've got at me. It's rude."

"Yeah, leave her alone," I said, unsuccessfully trying to sound tough.

"I don't like to be bossed around," the bodybuilder said.

He ran the knife alongside Rolvo. The scraping sounded like nails on a chalkboard.

"Hey!" I was surprised to find the cherry slush bomb in my hand. Before I knew what was happening, I tossed it at the truck. Slowly, it ran down the windshield.

"Uh-oh," the bodybuilder said, feigning fear. "My brother's not going to like that. He just washed the truck today."

"Look, I don't want any trouble," I said, wincing when my voice cracked.

The truck's windshield wipers turned on and pushed my cherry slush bomb back and forth. Back and forth. Then the driver's side window of the truck rolled down. I could see a man drinking a beer. He raised it to me. "Just let me finish this," he said. "Then I'll beat the shit out of you."

He opened the truck door, crushed the beer can, and got out. For a moment, I was confused.

"Twins," Monarch said admiringly. "Twin assholes."

Twin #2 had crazy eyes. My throat went dry. Monarch jumped into Rolvo, but before I could do the same, the two men strode toward me, blocking my way.

"Lock the doors," I yelled to Monarch before sprinting away from the iffy Mart and into the night.

Day 3

CHAPTER 38

They were fast, but I was faster. I could hear shouting behind me, but I kept going, refusing to turn around. I had to make a split-second decision — run into the Brookhaven woods or into the industrial section of town. I chose the latter, where there was a better chance of running into someone who could help me.

I was operating on pure adrenaline as I wove through the deserted alleyways, and past dilapidated buildings. Angry dogs with sharp teeth lunged from behind chain-link fences. It felt like a ghost town devoid of humans. I ran and ran and ran. After a while, it felt like I'd been running in circles. Finally, I slowed down. I was out of breath. I wished I had that cherry slush bomb now. My lungs were about to burst. It was only after I turned the corner and looked behind me that I realized I'd lost them. I'd never felt so good to lose something in my life.

I crouched over with my hands on my knees to catch my breath. Sweat dripped from my forehead onto the pavement. That's when I saw a pair of boots come into view.

Shit.

I looked up to see Twin #1 with a smug look plastered across his broad face. He was holding my empty slush cup.

"Say, smart mouth," he said. "I think it's time that you and me ought to have a little talk about your future — or lack of one."

I'd never been in a real fight before. However, something told me that was about to change.

"Strip," he ordered.

"Excuse me?"

"Strip," he said again.

"You're nuts," I told him.

"No, *your* nuts!" he joked before kicking me in the balls.

It was the most horrendous pain I had ever felt — like getting the wind knocked out of me, only a hundred times worse. I doubled over in agony as I staggered like a drunk.

He motioned to his brother and said, "By the way, he's won a lot of mixed martial arts bouts. Show him your tattoos."

Twin #2 obliged by taking off his T-shirt. Practically his entire body was covered in ink. Under the ink were muscles that were so big they looked like they should have their own nicknames.

"Strip," he said again.

I took off everything but my shoes and my boxers.

"That's a good boy," Twin #1 told me.

I was praying they would leave me alone. They had humiliated me enough.

I was wrong.

The first punch hurt the hardest. That was, until the second punch.

At least they were fair. They only pummeled me one at a time, and honestly, getting hit by Twin #1 was like a vacation compared to getting beat up by Twin #2.

I could feel sweat running down my face. Or was it blood? I couldn't tell.

This is how I am going to die, I thought.

I fought back, giving no thought to strategy, just swinging blindly. I wasn't landing many of my punches, and when I did, it probably hurt my fist more than it hurt my target.

This is how I am going to die, I thought.

I had never felt so much physical pain in my life.

This is how I am going to die, I thought.

Then something weird happened. With every blow they landed, I took it. I stopped fighting back and instead thought about the list of people who hated me, and all the shit-assed things I had done in my life. Maybe this was my punishment. Maybe I was getting what I deserved.

This is how I am going to die, I thought.

It's hard to gauge time when you are being thrashed — A minute? An hour? A week? A lifetime? But after a while, it seemed like my assailants were losing their oomph. Or had I just become accustomed to the hits and kicks? Whatever was happening, I felt totally numb.

This is how I am going to die, I thought, and I didn't care. Then I remembered my mother. Jeffrey's death nearly killed her. I didn't think she could take losing two sons.

Out of nowhere, a slow rage began to build until I couldn't contain it anymore. Like the Incredible Hulk, I stood up and roared. It was so loud that it scared them, and me. I must have looked like a maniac.

"Come on, hit me again," I said, spitting something out. "Do it and you'll die!"

I saw a flash of uncertainty in their eyes. I was used to seeing that during debate tournaments when I was about to obliterate my opponents, but this was different. In debate, I used my words. I used reasoning and logic. None of that mattered here.

"Let's leave," Twin #1 said to #2. "This is getting boring."

"Hit me!" I ordered. "Hit me! Hit me! Come on, hit me!"

Both laughed nervously.

The power of crazy.

I roared again and again as I watched them run away. Or, wait. They were still there? I swear, I could see Twin #1, and Twin #2, and Twin #3, and Twin #4. I saw a whole army of twins before I collapsed with my face planted against the asphalt.

It hurt to open my eyes, but when I did, I saw a penny. It looked out of place. My hand trembled. Every part of my body hurt. I inched my fingers toward the lucky penny, but before I could pick it up, my world went dark.

Day 3

CHAPTER 39

Higgs? Higgs! HIGGS!!!"

Huh? What? Someone was calling my name. But who?

"Have you seen my penny?" I asked.

I looked up at an angel.

She was beautiful. I must be in heaven, I thought.

"Oh my god, Higgs. You scared the hell out of me. I thought you were dead."

"Monarch?"

My left eye refused to open.

"Of course it's me," Monarch said tenderly. "You look like shit."

"Thank you."

"Wait here," she said.

"Don't leave me," I begged.

Monarch was gone for so long I thought I had dreamed her. I shut my eyes again. Every part of me hurt.

When I heard a car engine, I panicked. They were back.

It wasn't them.

Monarch held my head gently in her lap as she poured some water into my mouth. It took me a moment to realize that the metallic taste was blood. My blood.

"Where's Stuart?" I asked. "Stuart!!!!" I shouted.

"Calm down," Monarch said, shaking her head. "He's in the shoe box. He's safe. Higgs, where are your clothes?"

It was hard for me to talk. "Don't know."

Monarch ripped off the hem of her dress.

"Whoa," I said. "I'm not sure if now's the time for us to be doing this — but if you insist . . ."

She didn't try to stop me when I put my hand on her leg.

"I see they didn't touch your brain," Monarch said as she dampened the cloth and gently dabbed my face. "You're still an idiot."

"Ouch!"

"You're going to have a really impressive shiner and your lip is split." Monarch leaned in and used the cloth to soak up some of the blood. "Looks like your front tooth is chipped."

She smelled like sunshine.

Monarch was inches away from me when I took her face in my hands. Her skin was soft. She started to say something, but before she could get the first word out, I kissed her hard on the mouth. It killed my lips, but I didn't care. I could feel my heart racing, and even though moments before I thought I was going to die, suddenly it felt like everything was right in the world.

"Not awful," Monarch announced when we finally came up for air.

Her kisses tasted like cigarettes and chocolate and coffee. I wanted seconds, but she pushed me away.

"Listen, Higgs Boson Bing," she said affectionately. "That didn't mean anything, okay? So don't go getting all mushy on me or anything, got it?"

I didn't blink. My sight was slowly coming back. Monarch looked all gauzy. Without taking her eyes off me, she took an endless drag on her cigarette and released the most amazing series of smoke rings.

I was in love.

"Oh god, not again. Stop staring at me like that," Monarch said, swatting me away. "It's creepy."

I couldn't stop grinning. I was in pain from the beating, yet felt oddly energized.

"May I kiss you again?" I asked, leaning into her. I felt dizzy.

"No you may not," Monarch said. "I told you, that didn't mean anything."

She was wrong about that.

Monarch looked me over then asked, "Do you think you can walk?"

I nodded as she helped me up. Even though I could make it without her, I held on tight as I hobbled toward Rolvo.

The stars were out.

"How did you find me?" I asked.

"Is that your bonus question?"

I shook my head.

"Here," she said, holding out the Robe of Depression. "You don't want to bleed all over the upholstery."

It was only then that I realized that all I had on were shoes and boxers. The twins had stolen my clothes. I slipped the robe on. There was something hard in one of the pockets. I was surprised to find a miniature Rubik's Cube. It must have been one of Jeffrey's.

As Monarch drove, I listened to the hum of the engine. My body was sore, but in a weird way, it felt good. It reminded me that I was alive. I offered Stuart a piece of cheese. Monarch was gripping the steering wheel with both hands. Her eyes were on the road and she looked solemn.

"Where are we going?" I asked.

"The game is over," she said, staring straight ahead. "I'm taking you to the emergency room."

I started to shake my head, but it hurt too much. "No," I said. "I'm fine."

"You are not. You're hurt," Monarch said.

"Really, I'm okay," I insisted. I didn't want that night to end — certainly not in the hospital, where they'd probably call my parents. "I've never felt better," I insisted. "I swear."

This made her smile, and suddenly, it was true.

"Let's go take a look at you, and if nothing's broken, we can skip the ER," she said. "I hate hospitals."

The roads cleared and trees popped up. Monarch pulled into a rest stop and I made my way into the bathroom. The glare killed my eyes. I blinked back the bare lightbulb, and when I did, I screamed. I turned from side to side and examined myself in the dirty mirror. My face was battered and swollen. A black eye was starting to form and there was blood caked near my mouth.

It took a couple of turns of the sink handles to get the water running, but when it started, it came in cold and clean. It stung when I splashed water on my face. Red swirled in the sink before running down the drain. I was determined to wash away all traces of the twins. When I was done, my face still looked like a punching bag. Part of my front tooth was missing. My balls ached. The welts on my chest would soon turn as dark as the tattoos on Twin #2's body.

I slipped Mom's pink bathrobe back on to hide the bruises.

As I ran my tongue up against the edge of my cracked tooth, it felt sharp and dangerous. The twins may not have killed me, but my father surely would.

"A dentist has to have perfect teeth. We are our own best advertising."

Ever since I announced that I wanted to be a dentist, my dad started giving me pointers and tips. He'd regale me with stories about work. What he was saying was not important. I just liked that he was talking to me the way he used to talk to Jeffrey. So what if the sight of blood made me want to faint, or that looking for tooth decay and rot was repulsive. I could get over it.

I got back in the car and took Stuart out of his box. He squirmed in my hands and it felt as if our racing hearts were synchronized.

As Monarch maneuvered Rolvo through the hills in the newer part of Monte Vista, I glanced at the mini mansions. These people had serious money. Rolvo idled across the street from an imposing two-story house. It was all glass and steel. There was a "Welcome Home" banner draped over the front door. Monarch just stared at it. I thought about the battered trailer that she lived in, so far removed from a house like this.

"Why are we here?" I asked.

A small, sad smile crossed her lips. "I could ask myself that," she said cryptically. She hit the gas. "Let's get out of here," she said.

I turned on the radio. The Wanton Weasels were wailing out "Kill Me Now and Forever." Monarch changed the channel to classical. Pachelbel's Canon in D Major. It was my mother's favorite. I wondered what she was doing right then, and how she was going to handle Dad leaving her. Everyone was leaving her.

"This is Pachelbel," I told Monarch.

"I know," she said.

At first I was surprised. She didn't seem like a classical music sort of person. But by then, I had begun to suspect that Monarch was full of surprises, and I was right.

Day 3

CHAPTER 40

I gave Monarch directions to a tidy faux Tudor house with a familiar battered white VW Beetle parked in front of it. There was a "Tuba or Not Tuba" sticker on the bumper and a crooked USC decal on the rear window.

My phone, and my wallet, had been in my pants pocket, so I couldn't call Nick. I didn't want to risk ringing the doorbell and waking Mrs. Milgram, so instead I threw rocks at his bedroom window. It seemed like forever, but finally Nick pulled back the curtains.

"Holy father of God!" he cried when he came outside and saw me. "What happened? It looks like you hit a herd of buffalo."

"There was an incident with a cherry slush bomb," I told him. Nick looked confused. "I pissed some guys off. I got beat up," I explained. My eye hurt every time I blinked and my entire body was so sore that I couldn't isolate the pain.

"Why are you wearing that?" Nick asked, gesturing to the bathrobe. "And why are you holding a mouse?"

"It's a long story." I said. "Can I borrow some clothes?"

"Sure, whatever," he said.

"And I need some money too."

Nick nodded. He was like that, always there when you needed him. Accepting to a fault.

"Hey Nick," I began. Something had been bothering me. "All those years of me taking the credit for your work, if it bothered you so much, why didn't you say anything?"

He shook his head. "I don't know. It was so gradual, and you were so good at letting people think it was all you, and I . . . I was, I guess I was content to be in your shadow."

"Shit, Nick. You should have said something. I mean, you told Samantha, so I know it must have really bothered you."

He shrugged. "I did tell you a couple of times, but I guess you didn't hear me."

"When did you ever tell me?"

"Plenty of times," Nick insisted.

"Give me an example."

"After state finals, I said, 'I'm so glad I worked so hard on those briefs, I think they clenched us the title.' And you said, 'Yeah, we won again!'"

"And . . . ?"

"And you didn't say, 'Hey thanks, Nick. You did a great job, we couldn't have won without your hard work.'"

"I'm supposed to say stuff like that? I thought you knew."

"How can I know if you don't tell me . . . ?"

I felt like I was arguing with Roo.

"AH-HEM!!!"

Startled, Nick and I looked over at Rolvo.

"This chatfest is all very lovely," Monarch said, getting out and stretching her arms above her head. "But I have to pee."

Nick's jaw dropped.

"Mr. Bing, where are your manners?" Monarch said coyly as she slowly circled Nick. "Who's this well-dressed young man?"

When Monarch winked at Nick, I noticed that he was wearing blue plaid pajamas. As long as I've known him, he's worn pajamas to bed. Even on debate trips when the other guys slept in T-shirts and boxers, there was Nick in his pajamas. The weird thing was that they've always been those exact same blue plaid pajamas, just in bigger and bigger sizes.

Nick looked scared. He didn't move, as if afraid that Monarch would attack. Knowing her, she might have.

"Oh, excuse me. Monarch, this is Nicholas 'Nick' Milgram, my best friend. Nick, this is Monarch, no last name, my . . . my . . ."

She reached out and shook his hand so hard that his head bobbled. "I'm Higgs's muse," she announced. "Now, tell me, Mr. Milgram, do you happen to have a bathroom inside that lovely house of yours?"

"Through the door, to the left," he said robotically. "But don't wake my mom."

"I thank you," Monarch said. She gifted him with a smile. "And my bladder thanks you."

Nick and I watched as she galumphed toward his house. When Monarch disappeared inside, he turned to me, his eyes wide. "What the hell was that?!!!"

"Monarch," I said, trying to sound nonchalant. "My muse. She lives in the woods."

He shook his head as if trying to decipher what I had just told him. "She lives in the woods? What, like some sort of fairy goblin or Hobbit?"

"Something like that. It's really hard to explain."

Nick began bouncing up and down on his toes. He did this when we were debating too. The competition thought it was to throw them off, but really, it was how he stayed focused.

"Are you two — together?" he asked.

"That's the best cross-ex you can come up with?"

"Well," he said, throwing me an evil grin, "clearly I'm no Higgs Boson Bing, first speaker."

I laughed. I had missed Nick so much. "No, we're not together in the Biblical sense if that's what you're getting at."

"Thought so," he said. "She doesn't seem your type."

"What exactly is my type?" I wondered out loud.

"Beauty queen-ish," he started to say, "like Roo . . ."

Just then, Monarch came out of the house. She was carrying an armful of water bottles, a loaf of bread, plus a couple of towels, a potted plant, and a Popsicle. "I hope you don't mind if I borrow these," she said. "I found them in the kitchen."

Clearly flustered, Nick began to blink rapidly. "Oh, sure," he told her. "Yeah, uh, help yourself. Sure. Okay. Yeah. Take whatever you want. Yes."

And that was why I was a better debate speaker than Nick Milgram.

Monarch handed me the Popsicle. "Here, Higgs." When I started to unwrap it, she stopped me. "It's not to eat. Put it on your eye, it'll help stop the swelling.

"We would love to stay and chat," Monarch was saying to Nick as she played with his hair. He was frozen stiff and blinking rapidly. "But it could be dangerous to stay here. I saw it on the news." Monarch lowered her voice to imitate a news anchor, "Mice on the loose at Monte Vista Mall."

"You saw it on the news?" I asked.

"You heard me. Someone shot a video of the mice running around." She turned to Nick. "By the way, that's some big-assed TV you have."

He blushed.

"Is anyone recognizable on the video?" I asked.

Monarch shook her head. "Only if you know who you're looking for."

"What are we talking about?" Nick asked.

"Higgs, c'mon, we gotta go," Monarch said, trying to make her voice sound small and scared, but not succeeding. "There are bad guys on the loose."

"You don't have anything to worry about," Nick assured her. "This is a really safe area."

"Really, Nick. Is that so?" Monarch said. "No troublemakers of any kind?"

"No," he said sincerely. "We have neighborhood watch."

I tried to suppress a grin.

"Nick," I said, "will you text my mom? Tell her my cell phone battery is dead, but I'm staying at your house, and remind her there's no school for seniors tomorrow."

He looked at me, then Monarch, then back at me. Then it was time for Nick to suppress a grin. "Sure thing," he said as Monarch and I got in Rolvo.

It wasn't until we were a couple miles away that I suddenly remembered why we had gone to Nick's in the first place.

"Go back," I said.

"Why?"

"Because I forgot the clothes and the money."

"Forget it," Monarch said, stepping on the gas. "Not worth it. Never go back. Besides, you look sexy in a pink bathrobe."

Friday

Day 2

CHAPTER 41

I awoke confused. It took me a while to figure out that I was in the Airstream. My back ached and there was a serious crick in my neck. My entire body felt battered and I had a killer hangover, though I couldn't even recall drinking. As I slowly sat up, I made old-man noises — the kind of grunts that came out of my dad when he spent the night on the couch.

"Monarch?" I called out.

There was no answer. The pink bathrobe was wadded up in the corner next to my shoes. I was naked, and couldn't find my boxers anywhere. What time was it? I needed to take a piss. I slipped on the bathrobe and went outside. Rolvo's keys were gone and so was Monarch.

Without a phone, wheels, or clothes, there wasn't much I could do. So I waited, and waited. At least I had Stuart to keep me company. I lifted him out of his box and nuzzled him. He really was an exceptional mouse. Gentle, smart, loyal. Everything you could ask for in a pet, or a friend. As Stuart timidly explored the trailer, I picked up Monarch's copy of *Les Misérables*. It was in French, so I couldn't read it. Instead, I began *On the Road*.

Forty pages into the book, Monarch showed up carrying two big bags. She was singing a Wonton Weasels song. One bag was full of groceries, the other was from La Mode, an upscale department store.

I pulled the bathrobe tighter around my waist, but it barely closed.

"Here," she said, tossing the La Mode bag to me. She took out tins of oysters, crackers, chocolates, and a newspaper from the other bag.

"You read the newspaper?" I asked. I was starving.

Monarch looked insulted, then admitted, "I read the comics. Put on some clothes." She motioned to the La Mode bag. Inside were boxers, socks, a T-shirt, and running shorts.

"Turn around," I told her as I took off the robe and put on the clothes.

"Oooh, suddenly modest, are we?" she asked flirtatiously.

"Did we . . . ? Did you and I . . . ? Last night . . . ?"

Monarch let go of one of her deep, throaty laughs. "If we had, you would have remembered," she assured me.

We both blushed.

"I don't remember much, except for being beat up, and then going to Nick's," I admitted. "And, um, why was I naked?"

"You peed in your underwear," Monarch said.

I wished I hadn't asked.

"Higgs, you were hurting and in total denial. So I gave you a double dose of pain killers and they knocked you out."

"Pain killers? Where did those come from?"

"Courtesy of Angela M. Milgram."

"Nick's mother gave them to you?"

"Nope," Monarch said as she expertly opened the oyster tin. "I took them from the medicine cabinet."

I looked down at my new clothes and the food Monarch was putting on paper plates. Suddenly, I wasn't hungry. "Where did you get the money for all that?" I asked. "You didn't steal from Nick's mom did you?"

"No," Monarch said defensively. "Jesus, Higgs. Have some faith in me."

"So how did you pay for all this stuff?"

She opened the Airstream door. Her back was to me, and her shoulders looked tense. Monarch took a deep breath, and I watched as her entire body relaxed. "I pawned the necklace," she said, turning to face me.

I felt like I had been hit again.

"You can't do that," I protested.

"I just did," Monarch said defiantly. "You gave it to me. It belonged to me."

I slumped down against the side of the trailer. "Maybe I'd better go home," I told her.

"Why? I thought we were having fun."

"This isn't right," I said. "My mom might be worried about me. Plus, I have to take care of that whole Harvard thing. You might not understand this, but Harvard is what I've been working toward most of my life. If I don't go, my parents are going to flip out."

Monarch looked serious for a change. "I do know how you feel," she said, picking at one of the croissants. "Higgs, there's something I should tell you —"

"What?"

"I . . . I . . . All this talk about you, and college, and well, you see . . ." Monarch's voice trailed off and suddenly she looked different. Less self-assured. Nervous. She began to absentmindedly turn the pages of the newspaper on the counter. "You see, Higgs," Monarch hesitated. "There's something I need to tell you."

I stood up straighter, which was hard to do in an Airstream. "Yes?"

"I'm not . . . I'm not . . . I'm not . . . Audrey Hepburn!" Monarch yelped. "There's an Audrey Hepburn film festival playing over in Rancho Rosetta. We HAVE to go to that!" she said, pointing to the newspaper.

"That's what you wanted to tell me?" I was more than mildly disappointed. I had thought she was going to tell me some incredible secret. The kind where if you betrayed it, you could be killed.

Monarch was still talking. "You don't have school, that's all done. Neither one of us wants to be cooped up in this tin can right now. And it's *Audrey Hepburn*."

"Audrey who?"

"Come on. You might learn a thing or two."

"What about Stuart?"

"He'll be fine here," Monarch said, grabbing my hand. "Come on, we're going to the movies!"

Day 2

CHAPTER 42

Roman Holiday had already started. "That's Audrey Hepburn," Monarch explained as we settled in. There was a waiflike girl on the screen. "She's a princess pretending to be a commoner. Gregory Peck is a reporter. He knows she's a fraud, but he plays along to get a good story. Plus, he's crushing on her."

I shook my head. "I'm not into this sort of —"

Before I could finish, Monarch cut me off. "Higgs," she said, "Chill. Stop worrying about the world and escape for a while."

That might have been the best advice I ever got. I settled into my seat, but I wasn't watching the film, I was watching Monarch. Even in the dark, I could see her eyes sparkling. It was just Monarch and me, and Audrey Hepburn and Atticus Finch. A double date.

As the movie wore on, I put my arm around Monarch, and when she didn't slug me, I was glad that the theater was dark so no one could see me smiling. With all the shit going on in my life, she was the one good thing keeping me afloat and I wasn't about to let go of her.

I nuzzled her neck and then kissed her as Audrey Hepburn put her hand into a statue called the Mouth of Truth.

Monarch laughed as she swatted me away. Not exactly the response I was hoping for. But it wasn't a flat-out rejection either. "Stop it," she said, laughing. "I'm trying to watch the movie."

I didn't try to kiss her again, but as a concession, I kept my arm around her, delighted that she let me.

As the credits rolled, Monarch stared at the screen, unmoving. The lights came on and I looked at her, surprised. "You're crying!" I said.

"I am not," she said, wiping her face with the back of her hand. "I have allergies."

"No, no, you are crying," I insisted.

"I AM NOT CRYING," Monarch shouted before running out of the theater.

I found Monarch in the parking lot, leaning up against Rolvo and puffing on a cigarette.

"I wasn't crying," she said defensively. There were makeup smudges under her eyes.

"I know," I said, adding, "I love you."

"What?"

"You heard me." She wasn't going to make this easy.

"Wow, those guys who beat you up really rattled your brain," Monarch said. She blew her nose loudly, and then wiped her eyes with the back of her hand.

"I love you."

"Seriously, Higgs, stop saying that. It's getting annoying. I mean, really. How can you mean it when we've only known each other for four days?"

"Five days," I corrected her. "And I just know."

"How? Explain."

"Audrey Hepburn and Gregory Peck fell in love in less time than we've known each other," I said.

When Monarch opened her mouth and no words came out, I won my point. For someone who came off as so tough, she had a soft spot.

"So, what did you think of the movie?" she asked, leaning toward me. "Didn't you love it?"

"It was okay."

"Okay?" she croaked. "The princess went on an adventure that she will never forgot. She stepped out from behind the repressive life that was cast for her and had a glorious lark."

"And then back to her responsibilities when it was over," I reminded Monarch. "It wasn't a happy ending."

"She was bound by duty to her family, and her fate had been cast at birth," she parried. "What she did was admirable. It was bittersweet and she should be applauded for her loyalty to family. It was her destiny."

"It wasn't a happy ending," I repeated.

Day 2

CHAPTER 43

You okay?" I asked.

Monarch was tired of driving, so I was at the wheel.

"We've had a pretty good time together, haven't we?" she said, sounding far away.

"It wasn't awful," I said, when what I really meant was that, despite all the shit that had gone down, it had been the best week of my life.

This made Monarch laugh. I was about to tell her that I loved her again, but I didn't want to risk pissing her off. Monarch's mood had shifted, and she turned and faced the window, not saying a word for the rest of the ride.

Later, as we walked across the gravel pit, there was a sadness in the air that I could not place. Monarch didn't seem like herself. She was unusually quiet, and once when I tripped, she didn't even make fun of me.

"Big day for you tomorrow, isn't it?" Monarch finally said as more of a statement than a question. "High school seniors all over the country are graduating."

"Graduation *and* my Harvard interview," I reminded her. "Time to suck it up."

It was dark. My heart skipped a beat when Monarch slipped her arm through mine. Her steps slowed. "Yeah, reality sucks," she said, sounding bitter.

I don't know why I was surprised to hear this. I guess I had admired the way she was living, without anyone or anything to be accountable to. Carefree. But when I really thought about it — living in a trailer with no electricity, no running water, no income — maybe it wasn't so wonderful after all. I wondered how long Monarch had been on her own. It couldn't have been easy.

"You don't have to live like you do," I ventured. She raised an eyebrow. "I mean, what if you went back to school, graduated, got a job? Maybe even went to college. Clearly, you're smart."

Monarch snorted. "What — so I can be a dentist like you and cure the world of gingivitis? Is that your definition of happiness? What's in it for you, other than making your father happy?"

"It's what I want to do," I said. It sounded like someone else talking. "I mean, I've always wanted to be a dentist. Sure. Yeah, it's what I want."

If this had been a debate, my opponent would have surely caught the hesitancy in my response and annihilated me.

"And Harvard," Monarch asked. "That's your dream too?"

"Yes, Harvard," I said, aware that I had made it sound more like a question than an answer.

"Well, what's your definition of happiness, then?" I said quickly.

In debate, when you don't have a solid answer to your opponent's line of questioning, you redirect the subject.

Monarch stopped walking. "You really want to know?"

I nodded.

"I'd love to be an actress," she confided. Monarch looked deliriously happy when she said this. "Slipping in and out of roles, and getting paid for it. But that'll never happen."

"Why not?

"Because" was all she said, in a way that told me the conversation was closed.

I wondered if she would be any good at acting. I didn't think so. I couldn't imagine Monarch being anyone but herself.

"Wait here," she said when her trailer was in sight. Monarch left me standing next to a rotted-out tree stump. After a couple of minutes, she came out of the trailer carrying Stuart's box and with the Robe of Depression draped over her arm. "These are yours."

"You're acting like we're never going to see each other again," I joked. When she didn't smile, my mouth suddenly went dry. "Wait. You are planning on never seeing me again, aren't you?"

Monarch just shook her head. "We had fun. We had laughs. And now it's over. You go your way and I'll go mine."

"I . . . I don't understand. Was it something I said? Something I did?"

"Didn't you pay any attention to the movie?" Monarch asked.

"What movie? *Roman Holiday*? Okay, I am officially confused."

"Poor sweet Higgs," Monarch said. She ran her finger across my lips. "The clock is striking midnight and it's time to turn back into a pumpkin. Farewell, Higgs Boson Bing."

I wasn't ready for midnight. I wasn't ready to leave Monarch, or to face whatever was waiting for me at home. I scrambled to think of an excuse to stretch the evening out. If I could buy some more time, I could convince Monarch to keep seeing me and prolong my future. I wasn't a champion debater for nothing.

"Stuart," I said, gently taking him out of the box. "Poor little thing. You helped save his life, and now you want to leave him. Imagine what he must be thinking."

"He must be thinking that it's time for a snack," she said.

"Let's take him for one last walk together," I said. "He'd like that."

"You'd like that," Monarch volleyed back.

"We'd like that," I said.

I held Stuart in front of her face. Neither moved. Finally, Stuart let out a small squeak, and when Monarch tried not to smile, I knew I had her. "Fine. C'mon, Higgs. Let's take this mouse for a walk." She flung the Robe of Depression around her shoulders like a cape, but then tossed it to me. "It looks better on you than me," she said.

I handed Stuart over as I slipped on the robe. I wasn't about to argue with her.

We hiked up the hill in contented silence. I never wanted the night to end. After a while, we stopped to sit and rest against a fallen tree. As Stuart nestled more deeply into the robe, Monarch leaned against me and shut her eyes. I wasn't about to wake her. Whatever dream she was having, I hoped I was in it.

I'm not sure how much time had passed, or when I fell asleep, but I awoke to Monarch poking me in the ribs. "Time to go home, Higgs," she was saying.

"No, no," I corrected her as I stood. "We need to make it to the top of the hill."

"Higgs, I'm tired," Monarch said, stretching.

"Please," I said. "We're almost there."

She shook her head, but we kept going, hand in hand, and I was happy — that is, until we neared the top.

"Holy shit!" I cried.

Hanging off the side of the water tower was a banner of Hitler Higgs.

"Wow," Monarch said. "It really does look like you."

I was speechless.

"Listen, Higgs Boson Bing," she continued as I stared, unable to speak. "I have a few things to say to you. It's been fun being your buddy, but we're going to say good-bye, here. After tonight, you need to go back to your fancy life and your fancy college and the world that you and your parents have mapped out for you. You can't be hanging out around here, slumming it."

"I'm not slumming it," I told her. I could not take my eyes off the banner. "I want to be here. With you."

"No you don't."

"Yes, I do."

"No, you don't.

"You're wrong."

"Prove it," Monarch said.

"How?"

Monarch's eyes lit up, and from the way her lips curled into a mischievous smile, I knew that I was in trouble.

"Take the banner down," she said. "I know it's killing you to see it."

I felt myself pale.

"But . . . but . . . but it's up there. On the water tower," I stammered.

"Thought so," she said. "I know your type. You're all talk."

Monarch handed Stuart back to me, turned around, and started heading downhill. As I watched her leave, I thought about whomever it was who was trying to destroy me. I thought about all the shit that was my life. But mostly I thought about Monarch.

My stomach started to flip, and against my better judgment, I heard myself calling after her. "Wait, Monarch, come back. I'll do it!"

Day 2

CHAPTER 44

Shit, damn, shit, damn, shit, damn Monarch. Why did I let her talk me into this, I thought.

Don't look down.

Don't look down.

Don't look down.

I can't look down, I told myself.

If I looked down, I'd freak out, lose my grip, let go, plummet to the ground, and die. But that would mean that Stuart would die too. I checked to make sure he was still there. I was lucky that the Robe of Depression was so thick and had deep pockets to keep him from falling out.

Shit, damn.

"Higgs," Monarch said, sounding bored. "You're not even five feet off the ground."

"Shut up," I snapped. "I've got everything under control."

I should have given Stuart to Monarch to hold.

She was laughing. I used to think her throaty laugh sounded sexy, but I changed my mind. It sounded deranged.

"Listen, Higgs, I was just testing you. You passed, okay? You don't have to climb up the water tower. Five feet is fine," she said. "Come on down."

"No," I told her, despite the voice in my head shouting, "Get down!"

"Come on, Higgs," Monarch said again, adding coyly, "Climb down. I'll make it worth your while."

I hesitated, wondering what "worth you while" meant, but then said stubbornly, "No." I was going to climb that water tower if it killed me.

"If you come down now, I'll let you see my hidden tattoo . . . ," she teased.

Monarch had a hidden tattoo?

"No," I shouted stubbornly.

As I reached for the next rung, sweat dripped off my brow. My hands were clammy, making it hard to grip the ladder. The robe flapped open in the wind. Still, I was determined to reach the top. It was taking forever, and every step up felt like certain death. But I was not going to let whoever put Hitler Higgs up win. It was me against the banner. Breathe. Remember to breathe. It wasn't so bad.

After I made it over halfway up, I actually started to feel good. Confident. I was in control . . . until I looked down.

Everything started to spin. I saw Monarch over there, and over there, and over there. She was so small. "Stop moving," I yelled.

"I am standing still," she shouted back. "Come on down, Higgs. You've proven yourself!"

Maybe she was right. Maybe it was no big deal that there was a banner of my face with a Hitler mustache and horns. Maybe I should even be flattered that someone was so obsessed with me they'd do this. I stepped down, but then my foot slipped.

"M . . . M . . . Monarch?"

It took me a few seconds to regain my footing.

"Come down, Higgs!" she pleaded. "I never meant for you to go all the way to the top. It was just a joke."

Just a joke?

Before Jeffrey died, I used to be just a joke.

The metal ladder rungs were thin and increasingly hard to grip. Monarch kept yelling as I made my way up. My palms were sweaty. My heart was racing. Panic permeated every part of my body. Still, I kept going, like a madman, determined to succeed at any cost. Nothing could stop me. That is, until something tickled my arm.

Oh god.

I tried not to freak out. "Stuart, get back into my pocket," I ordered. "Get in there, NOW."

Perhaps it was because he had almost been a snack for a snake . . . or perhaps because he was too scared to move . . . or perhaps it was because Stuart Little was a mouse and didn't understand what I was saying, but whatever the case, he did not retreat back into the safety of the Robe of Depression. Instead, he jumped.

Day 2

CHAPTER 45

Nooooooooo!!!"
"Higgs? Higgs what's happening? Are you okay?" When
I didn't answer, Monarch shouted, "I'm coming up."

She must have had superhuman abilities, because before I
could tell her not to, Monarch was below me on the ladder. "Are
you all right?" she asked, out of breath. Then she looked down.
"Fuck, it's scary up here!"

"S-s-s-stuart j-j-j-j-jumped," I told her.

"Oh, Higgs." Monarch's voice broke. "I am so sorry."

We were both silent as we clung on to the ladder. For a
moment, the world stopped spinning.

"Come on down," she said gently. "I'll be here to catch you if
you fall."

"Okay," I said. I was exhausted. "I think it's time for me to
go home."

"Me too," she said softly.

As we both took slow, tentative steps down the metal rungs, I wondered if the wobbly ladder could support the weight of both of us. Suddenly, Monarch stopped and I almost stepped on her hand.

"Higgs?" she whispered reverently. "Higgs, look up."

When I did, I couldn't believe what I was seeing.

"Hickory, dickory, dock," Monarch said.

Stuart was climbing up the ladder.

"Stuart!" I ordered. "Come back here, right now."

Monarch chuckled. "You're not the boss of him, you know. Come on, Higgs, let's go home."

"No," I replied.

"No?"

"No, I'm not leaving without Stuart," I said.

"Hon, don't risk your life for him, he's just a mouse."

Just a mouse?

"Whoa, wait, what do you mean? That's Stuart up there. He's my friend and he's going to be all alone on the top of a water tower if I don't save him!"

"Calm down," she ordered. "Stop screaming."

"I AM NOT SCREAMING!"

Monarch raised an eyebrow.

"I am not screaming," I said.

"Listen, Stuart will be fine. It's you I'm worried about."

"Why? Do you think I'm a wimp who can't hack it up here?"

"Higgs," she said as if speaking to a child. "It's late. I'm tired. Graduation is tomorrow. It's scary up here and you're afraid of heights, and frankly, I think you're sounding a little crazed."

"You can go on down," I told Monarch. "But I'm not leaving without Stuart."

She shook her head. "All right, then, Higgs Boson Bing. It's been nice knowing you. You're on your own."

A narrow ledge circled the base of the tower. There was a short rail around it, but not much else in the way of safety. It was like a million miles straight up and I was near the top. I screwed my eyes shut. As long as I didn't look down, I'd be fine, I told myself. I focused on Stuart. He was making his way to the roof like a mouse on a mission. Maybe the mother ship was going to land and Stuart would be the first aboard. I would be second.

"Stuart!" I shouted. "Wait for me!"

Out of the corner of my eye, I saw the Hitler Higgs banner. I had almost forgotten that it was how this all started, with someone mocking me. And there I was, about to die while trying to rescue a mouse. I had saved him from the snake. Hopefully, I could save him from himself.

Slowly, I inched along the ledge toward the banner. I was that close. I might as well get rid of it. Two flimsy pieces of rope lashed the banner to the rail. With a hard yank, I untied the left side, then flattened myself again the tower and inched to the right side. The banner floated to the ground, back and forth like an oversized feather. That had been easier than I thought, but my next challenge would not be.

I couldn't see Stuart, but I knew he had made it to the very top. He was probably alone and scared. I know I was. The only way to the roof was via a narrow ladder with no safety cage around it. One hand over the other, I began my final climb. Monarch's screaming was drowned out by the wind and my fears.

My palms were sweaty. My legs were weak. Still, I headed up. I couldn't save everyone, but I could save Stuart.

"Stuart! Stuart," I cried, "don't move!"

Just then I heard a commotion.

"Let go of me!!!" Monarch was shouting.

I looked down to see her standing between two men. It was dark. Even with the light of the crescent moon, I couldn't make out who she was with. I prayed that it wasn't the twins who had tracked us down to exact revenge. I shuddered and almost slipped. A big bright light shone into my eyes. I had to hold one hand over my face to keep from being blinded. What sounded like the voice of God pierced the air.

"You in the pink bathrobe, this is the police. Come down NOW."

The police?

"Right now," the voice boomed. "You are illegally trespassing. Come down, NOW."

Day 2

CHAPTER 46

Slowly, I resumed my ascent.

"You are going the wrong way," the voice boomed. "Come DOWN."

I ignored him and didn't stop until I got to the very top. It was flatter than I thought it would be. I tried not to vomit. Deep breath. Take a deep breath, I told myself. I was feeling light-headed. Deep breath. I shut my eyes and when I opened them, I spotted Stuart standing still in the dead center of the water tower roof. He looked frail and frightened. One gust of wind could have blown him to a certain death. I was too chicken to walk to get him, so I crawled.

As if knowing I was coming to rescue him, Stuart was perfectly still. I cupped him in my hands. We were both shaking. In the distance, I could see my high school — bright lights illuminated the empty football field.

"Young man," the voice said, this time sounding kinder. "Come on down. Whatever happened can't be that bad."

What was he talking about? I wondered. What did he know?

"Don't jump," the voice said. "Don't jump."

Don't jump? Is that what they thought? That I was suicidal?

Gingerly, I inched my way back to the ladder. The ground seemed miles and miles away. Why was Monarch spinning? Was that a cop spinning with her? This was no time to dance. I gripped Stuart tight, then slipped him deep down into the safety of the bathrobe pocket. "Stay," I said. This time he did.

I felt sick again. Vomit rose in my throat. I pushed it back down, but not soon enough to erase the bitter acid taste that lingered in my mouth, a reminder of how fucked my life had become. Part of me wanted to hold on tight to something. Another part of me actually did want to jump. I could just let go right now, I thought. It would be so easy. Nothing had been easy for me before. But this seemed simple, until I thought about Jeffrey.

"Come down," the voice boomed. "Slowly."

"I ca . . . ca . . . can't," I said weakly. My hands shook. My grip was gone. Every time I tried to step down, my foot was suspended in air and I couldn't find the next rung. Terror seized me, and in one mad scramble, I was back on top of the water tower. I sat down as the panic paralyzed me. I had never been so tired in my life. It felt as if my entire body was shutting down.

"Just stay where you are," the voice said. "I'll come to you."

I wasn't going anywhere. I checked to make sure Stuart was still in my pocket.

He was.

In order to calm myself down, I fished around and retrieved Jeffrey's Rubik's Cube from the other pocket. I could hear his steady voice, telling me how to solve it. Telling me to slow down.

Relax. "Take your time, Higgs. Give it a chance and it'll all come together. Don't overthink it. Don't force it."

There. I did it. All the colors were the same on each side.

I set the Cube down. That's when I heard the voice again. "Higgs? Higgs Bing, is that you? Dude, what happened to you?"

A cop was walking slow and steady toward me. He had his hands up in the air as if he were surrendering. Something about him was familiar, and for a moment, I thought it was Jeffrey. My brother and his best friend were always watching police shows, and were obsessed with cops.

"Connor? Connor Douglas, is that you?" I asked, blinking hard.

He broke into a huge grin. "Yeah, man. It's me. Higgs, are you hurt?"

"I'm fine, Connor," I answered, even though I wasn't so sure about that.

"Are you trying to hurt yourself? From the look of your black eye and swollen lip, I'd say someone already tried to do the job. And that pink bathrobe? Nice touch."

I shook my head. "I'm not suicidal," I told Connor. "I'm scared of heights."

"I remember," he said. "Higgs, are you angry? Do you feel like hurting someone?"

I shook my head.

"Are you okay? Can you move? Can you walk?"

I nodded.

"Higgs," Connor said, "I gotta ask, what the hell are you doing up here?"

"I had to tear down the banner. It had my picture on it."

"It must have been one ugly picture!" Connor said. I recognized his laugh from when he and Jeffrey hung out together. They were always laughing. "Come on, Higgs. I gotta get you down."

"I can't, Connor," I said. "I can't go down that skinny ladder. I . . . I just . . ."

"Okay, okay, not a problem." Connor walked around the top of the water tower as casually as if he were on solid ground. He kept talking into the radio on his collar, but I couldn't hear what he was saying. Then he sat down next to me. "Man, look at that," Connor said, motioning toward the sunrise.

I looked at the giant orange sun rising over the city. It was beautiful.

We sat in silence for the longest time. "Am I going to jail?" I finally said.

Connor shrugged. "I don't know. Let's just get you down safe first, then we'll figure out the rest of this mess."

Just then the water tower started to shake.

Earthquake?

I looked down. Rolvo? I rubbed my eyes. It wasn't Rolvo. It was the real thing.

"Is there a fire?"

"No," Connor said, looking at the hook-and-ladder fire truck. "They're here to rescue you."

Saturday

Day 1

CHAPTER 47

The Rubik's Cube was still on top of the water tower. We were leaning on Connor's police car as his partner, an older guy, stood nearby, clearly bored. I cupped Stuart in my hands, determined never to let any harm come to him.

"Firemen and policemen," Monarch said, nodding approvingly. We were watching Connor talk to the firefighters and the EMTs. He was holding the banner. "Higgs, we ought to do this more often."

I ignored her.

"Hey," Monarch shouted. "Hey, cute cop guy!"

"His name is Officer Connor Douglas," I told her.

"Hey, Douglas, I could really use a smoke," Monarch yelled. "You got a cigarette?"

"Smoking's bad for your health," Connor said as he approached us.

"That's what I've been telling her!"

"You should listen to your boyfriend," he instructed Monarch as he put the banner in the trunk of the police car.

I didn't correct him.

"Did she do that to you?" he asked, pointing to my black eye.

"If I did, would you handcuff me?" Monarch purred.

Connor laughed. "Honey, you're dangerous," he told her.

I didn't like the way they were grinning at each other.

"When did you get back in town?" I asked. "I thought you moved to the Bay Area."

"I did," Connor said. "Did my training up there and worked in San Francisco for a couple of years, then put in for a transfer. I've only been back about a month. You two stay put. I've got to call this in."

I felt sick. I was in so much trouble. "I wonder why they thought I was trying to kill myself?" I said to Monarch.

"Because that's what I told them."

"That's crazy. Why would you say that?"

"Because it sounded more sane than you were trying to rescue your mouse."

She had a point. I held Stuart against my cheek.

"When was the last time you were really, really happy?" I asked.

"Two weeks ago," she said.

"What happened two weeks ago?"

"Two weeks ago I was in another place," Monarch said without explanation. "What about you, Higgs? When was the last time you were really, really happy?"

"Now. I'm really, really happy now."

Monarch kissed me on the cheek. "You are truly strange, do you know that?"

I took that as a compliment.

"Monarch . . . ," I began.

"Hmmm," she answered as she turned her attention toward the fire truck taking off. "Connor's cute, but I'm not one of those chicks who's into cops. However, firefighters are hot."

"Monarch, I love you," I blurted out.

"Oh, Higgs." Monarch ran her fingertips lightly across my face and I winced in pain. "That's so nice," she said, "and you're so sweet, but you're also full of shit. So please stop telling me you love me. It's getting annoying."

"I just told you that I loved you and your response is that I'm full of shit?"

Monarch looked proud of herself. "Yeah."

"Why?" I didn't even try to hide my hurt. "Why would you say something like that? What is wrong with you?"

"Look, you barely know me," she said. "If you knew the real me, I doubt you'd be saying that."

"I do know the real you."

"You only think you do. Listen, today is graduation. Then it's off to college. This is the end of the story for us."

Graduation. I had forgotten it was Saturday.

"I probably won't get into Harvard, remember?"

Monarch's face clouded. "Higgs," she said, sounding serious. "Don't screw up your life. Fix your mess. Ace your interview. Go to Harvard. It's what you were meant to do."

"Why are you of all people telling me this? I thought you

hated the Ivy League bourgeois. Are you thinking we don't belong together because we're so different?"

"It's because we're not," she said flatly.

To say that I was confused would be a monumental under-statement.

"Aw, Higgs, don't pout," she said.

When Monarch leaned in to give me a conciliatory kiss, I pushed her way. I didn't want her pity.

"Hey, is that any way to treat someone you love?" she teased.

Connor got off his radio and came around to us. "Sorry, but I need to take you two in."

"Why?" I asked. "I wasn't trying to hurt myself."

Connor's face turned grim. "Higgs, if you were trying to commit suicide, that's huge and you'll need to seek counseling. But if you weren't, not only did you trespass, but we had to call a rescue vehicle to get you down. Someone's got to pay for that. You'll be cited for causing public mischief and there are a whole lot of other charges that can be thrown at you."

"Public mischief," Monarch said, smirking. "Higgs, they got you for public mischief. What do you have to say for yourself?"

I couldn't speak.

Connor turned to face Monarch. "You're going to the station too."

"Excuse me, but no," Monarch said, her tone changing. "I have my rights. You have no reason to take me in."

"I could start with trespassing," he replied, "and I'm sure if I really started digging I could come up with more on you."

Like magic, Monarch was silenced.

The air was stilted. There were no door handles in the back of the police car, and there was no way to roll down the windows. Not that we could if we wanted to. Both Monarch and I were handcuffed. "Police procedure," Connor had explained apologetically.

"Seriously? Public mischief?" Monarch snorted as he started the engine. "You're a danger to society."

"Leave me alone," I told her. "Is everything a joke to you?"

"Not everything," she said.

Day 1

CHAPTER 48

The police station wasn't far, but the ride took forever. Monarch looked out the right window. I looked out the left. We were like two strangers who happened to be handcuffed in the back of a cop car. I could see Connor watching me in the rearview mirror as his partner drove in silence. I had finally overdosed on Monarch.

In the harsh light of the booking room, Monarch looked different. Younger, less confident.

"Higgs?" she called to me as she was being taken away.

I didn't answer her, even though it hurt.

Connor took away the tie to my bathrobe. "Empty your pockets," he said.

"I've got nothing," I told him.

The cell was a lot cleaner and nicer than the ones on television, and I was relieved to see that there was no four-hundred-pound tattooed guy who wanted to make me his girlfriend. Despite there being two bunk beds, a skinny old man was sleeping peacefully on the floor. He reeked of alcohol. Against the far wall was a metal toilet and sink. It smelled like day-old piss and fresh puke.

"You'll be here until we decide what to do with you," Connor told me. The drunk was snoring loudly. "Sorry about your roommate. He's harmless."

I was so glad that if I had to be hauled to the police station it was by my brother's best friend. "Connor," I asked, "how big a mess am I in?"

He shook his head. "With the law? Nothing a good lawyer couldn't get you out of. But from what I remember about your dad, he's not going to be happy about this."

"What about Monarch?"

"Who?"

"The girl I was with."

"I wouldn't worry about her, Higgs," he said, shaking his head. "That girl can take care of herself."

"Hey, Connor," I said as he started to head out. "Jeffrey would be proud that you're a cop."

He smiled. "He'd be proud of you too, Higgs. I heard you got into Harvard. It's what you've always wanted, right?"

"I wanted to go for Jeffrey," I said. "To honor his memory. Oh god, Connor, I've totally screwed up."

Connor let go of a deep sigh. "You think Jeffrey never messed up? He wasn't what your parents thought he was. Your brother was a regular guy who had too much to drink and fucked up. He was no saint, Higgs."

"He is now," I said. "Just ask my mom and dad. He would have been the third generation of Bing dentist."

Connor laughed. "Yeah, right. Jeffrey, a dentist."

"What?" I asked. "Why is that funny?"

"Your brother was only going to Harvard to make your parents happy. What he really wanted to do was be a cop. Everyone knew that."

"I didn't know that," I started to say.

"Why do you think he got so drunk after graduation?"

I let this sink in.

"Do what you want to do," Connor said. "That's what Jeffrey would have wanted. That's how you can honor him."

I lay down on the bunk bed. The mattress was hard, but I didn't care. I had a killer headache. A migraine times a million. My thoughts ricocheted. My stomach turned cartwheels. Every punch and kick, every name I had been called, all came back in a rush. I pulled Mom's Robe of Depression around me and allowed myself to be engulfed in its softness. I understood why it gave her comfort.

"Higgs Boson Bing!!!" Someone was shouting.

I bolted upright and instantly checked my pocket to make sure that I hadn't crushed Stuart. How long had I been asleep?

Stuart was gone.

Panic.

"There's a mouse in here!" the drunk slurred.

"We don't have mice," the policewoman said curtly.

I followed the drunk's sight line and spied Stuart under the sink. "I have to pee," I said.

When she turned around, I grabbed Stuart and slipped him back in my pocket.

"He has the mouse!" the drunk called out.

I flushed the toilet. "We can go now," I said.

"How come he gets to go . . . ," the drunk called out after me. "I love your coat — pink is your color!"

I followed the officer down the hall and into the lobby. My mother burst into tears when she saw me. She hugged me tight and then looked at my face and started crying again. "What did they do to you in there?" she asked. "Why are you wearing my bathrobe?"

I touched my lip. It still hurt. "I did this to myself," I told her. I didn't answer her second question.

My father's jaw looked absolutely locked. His gleaming smile was nowhere to be seen, and he looked much older than I had remembered him being. With him was a balding man with a briefcase. I wondered if it was not too late to run back and lock myself in the cell with the drunk.

"Higgs, are you all right? Why are you wearing your mother's bathrobe?" Dad asked. I stiffened when he hugged me. "What happened to your front tooth?"

"It's chipped," I said.

"Let me see that," my father said, examining my mouth. "We'll have to put a cap on that."

"Did this happen in jail?" the stranger asked, motioning to my face. He took out his cell phone and started taking photos. "We can sue the city."

"Higgs, this is your lawyer, John Dullaghan," Dad explained.

The policewoman looked like she was anxious for us to leave. She made me and my parents sign a bunch of papers.

"Am I free to go?" I asked.

"For now," she said.

"What's going to happen to Monarch?" I asked.

"Who?"

"Monarch, the girl I came in with."

"Oh, her," the policewoman said dismissively. "Her parents came and got her half an hour ago. There was quite a scene."

"Excuse me?"

"Her parents got her half an hour ago," she said again as she began stapling papers.

Her parents?

"Let's go, Higgs," my father told me.

Connor came out to say good-bye. "Mr. Bing," he said, extending his hand. "I haven't seen you in a while."

There was an awkward silence. After Jeffrey died, Connor would come by to talk to my mom. But it pained my father to see him, and it got so uncomfortable that after a while Connor stopped visiting.

"Connor," my father said, gripping his hand.

"So nice to see you again, Connor," Mom said, giving him a hug. She took a step back. "Let me look at you." Her eyes misted up.

Suddenly, Connor didn't look like a cop. He looked like the kid my big brother hung out with. I flashed back on the two of them wearing their LAPD badges and chasing imaginary bad guys. Now, though, there was only one police officer standing before me.

Mom nodded in approval as she stared at Connor, then gave him another hug. Dad coughed into his hand before turning away to hide his tears.

As I was guided out of the police station by my parents and my attorney, I ran back to thank Connor. He was carrying the Hitler Higgs banner.

"Why do you have that?" I asked.

"Just getting rid of it. You want it?"

"No way in hell . . . ," I started to say. Then I noticed something strange. My face burned red, and for a moment, I couldn't breathe.

I knew who had been trying to bring me down.

Day 1

CHAPTER 49

Outside, the sunlight was blinding. It had been the longest night of my life and all I wanted to do was to go home and sleep in my own bed. Nothing made sense — not that it ever did.

Monarch's parents picked her up? She said she didn't have parents. Had she lied to me? More likely, she had scammed the police by getting a couple people to pretend they were her parents. Still, I couldn't be sure. With Monarch, anything was possible.

"Higgs," my father said as he drove Mom's car. "Do you want to talk?"

Talking was the last thing I wanted to do.

"I have nothing to say," I told him.

"He's had a hard night," my mother intervened. "When Higgs is ready to talk to us, he will."

She gave me a reassuring smile, but I could tell she was worried. I noticed that my dad was wearing a suit and my mom was all dressed up. As we neared the high school, the parking lot was full. Then it hit me.

"I sort of thought I'd skip graduation," I announced.

I hadn't slept in twenty-four hours.

"You will do nothing of the sort," my father said. "You have a speech to give."

"That's right," Mom backed him up, and for a moment, they were a unified front. "I've brought your cap and gown."

I cupped Stuart in my hands so my parents couldn't see him.

"You've also got your phone interview with Harvard admissions," Dad reminded me. "Given your debate skills, you'll slide right through it. I'm not worried."

He might not have been worried, but I was. My future would be determined in a phone call.

As Mom started going over the details of my graduation party, I wondered what Monarch would have said if she could have heard her. There would be swans made out of ice, a live band, and a carving station with your choice of prime rib or turkey. However, if you were a vegetarian, like Monarch, there would be a sushi chef taking requests, and if you happened to be vegan, no problem, you would be well cared for too. My mother always thought of everything and everyone. Well, except for herself.

Knowing my father, the guest list would include many of his wealthier patients, his golf buddies, members of the local Harvard Alumni Association, and anyone who had ever served on city council. Would Mrs. Taelo be there? I wondered. Had Dad noticed the necklace was missing?

I slipped on the cap and gown, and made sure Stuart was safe. It was lucky that the shorts Monarch had bought for me had pockets. Was she back at her trailer? I wondered.

As we entered the football stadium, I was handed a program.

My name was still listed as a commencement speaker. The school orchestra was playing. Mr. Hermes looked funny in a suit. Charlie was wearing a dress. It was like some sort of alternative world. The bleachers on the football field were full of well-dressed friends and relations. The ceremony had already started. Before I went to join the senior class, Mom stopped me.

"Higgs," she said, softly. "Do you want to talk?"

"No."

"Higgs," my father said. He sounded worried. "I know I've put a lot of pressure on you lately, but, well, if any of this is my fault —"

My mother started crying. "Honey, were you going to jump off the water tower?"

Is that what they thought?

I shook my head. "No, Mom. I'd never do that," I assured her. "I was just trying to take down a stupid banner." Both had blank looks on their faces. "It was a prank on the seniors," I explained. I left out the part about Monarch and Stuart.

"See," Dad said to Mom. "You worry too much. I told you he's fine. Higgs knows he's going to ace that Harvard interview."

I started to say something, but instead I ran down the aisle toward the stage.

Zander Findley was seated next to Lauren Fujiyama, and Mr. Avis was next to her. Principal Kostantino was at the podium droning on about how we come into high school as children and leave adults. Lauren looked shocked to see me. She touched her eye and mouthed, "Are you okay?"

It was only then that I remembered my face had been used as a punching bag.

I nodded.

With no chair for me to sit in, I stood behind Zander.

"Nice of you to stop by," Mr. Avis said under his breath. "But you're not giving a speech. I believe we settled that."

I scanned the seniors and waved to Roo, who pretended not to see me. Nick gave me a thumbs-up and Samantha Verve gave me the finger. Rosalee was laughing at me. Mr. French stood near an exit, leaning on a broom.

"Our first speaker will be Lauren Anne Fujiyama," Principal Kostantino was saying, "and the closing speech of your high school careers will be delivered by Zander Rhodes Findley. Miss Fujiyama . . ."

There were cheers as Lauren stood, but before she could get to the microphone, I leaped up and blocked her. "What are you doing?" she asked, confused.

"It's okay," I told her with my hand over the mic. "Trust me. Please," I begged.

Lauren shook her head, but sat back down.

"Principal Kostantino, Mr. Avis, Lauren, Zander, parents, siblings, relatives, friends, and enemies, my name is Higgs Boson Bing."

"Dinky Dick!" someone yelled. Principal Kostantino stood and scanned the crowd for the perpetrator. Mr. Avis headed toward me, but Zander body-blocked him. "Let's hear what Higgs has to say," he said.

I nodded a thank-you to Zander, and continued. "During my four years at Sally Ride High School, I learned many things. Like what it feels like to be a winner."

I surveyed the audience. Most of the seniors were goofing off.

There was a beach ball being batted around. Paper airplanes punctuated the air. Those who were looking at me seemed bored. Still, I continued, "What I wished I had known earlier was that these are hollow victories without the respect of those who are my teammates and worthy opponents." Rosalee glared at me. Zander looked interested. Coach Valcorza nodded. My dad took pictures. I kept going.

"I was so focused on winning, that I lost sight of all that I had to lose and of who I am. Sure, I'm a winner . . . and a loser . . . and yes, even a Dinky Dick. If I've been a shit to you, I'm sorry." With that last line, there was a rumble through the crowd and suddenly everyone was paying attention. "If I have offended you, or stepped on you, or hurt you, I apologize. I mean that. I really do. This is not Higgs Boson Bing bullshitting you. This is me, Higgs, telling the truth, maybe for the first time in my life. Don't spend all your time trying to be someone you're not, because in the end you've got to live with yourself, and you might not like who you meet."

When I was done, there was silence, until Nick leaped up and started to cheer. We grinned at each other, and despite the spotty unenthusiastic applause from the crowd, I knew that however clumsy and ill thought out it had been, I had just delivered the best, most honest speech of my life.

Day 1

CHAPTER 50

Leaving was harder than expected. Everyone was running around hugging and screaming and crying, all at the same time. I had thought that I couldn't wait to leave high school, and now that the time was here, I found myself longing to stay.

"Come on, Higgs," my father insisted. "I had to pull a lot of strings to get someone to talk to you on a Saturday."

I couldn't move. It was as if I was anchored to the ground as everyone and everything swirled around me. Then I saw Roo. She was holding armloads of flowers and looked beautiful. I was about to approach her when my father put his arm around me and led me to the car.

"Wait up!"

It was Charlie. "Did you guys forget me?" she said, out of breath. She was lugging her cello. "You weren't going to leave without me, were you?"

"Of course not," my mother said, looking embarrassed.

"Did you mean all that stuff you said in your speech?" my father asked as he maneuvered down the road, weaving in and out of traffic despite being in Mom's minivan. Rolvo was still at the iffy Mart. And Dad's Porsche could only seat two.

"Yes," I told him.

"Well, it sounded funny to me. What was with the Dinky Dick stuff? Did someone dare you to say all those things? It wasn't the speech your mother and I were expecting."

It wasn't the speech I was expecting.

"Listen, Higgs," my father continued, "you have always had a way with words —"

No, I used to stutter, but you didn't notice me then, I wanted to say, but didn't.

Dad went on. "You just say whatever you need to and secure your place in Harvard. Make sure you reiterate that you are a legacy — the third generation of Bing at Harvard. If we need Dullaghan to step in and plead your case, he's ready. The man who will be interviewing you is named Kurt Boyle and he's a pushover. So tell him that not only did you start that animal whatever group, but that you donated a lot of your own money to it too. I can get my accountant to come up with some paperwork to back you up."

"What if Harvard rejects me?" I asked.

"Worse things could happen," Mom said.

Dad pulled the car over to the side of the road. He turned around and looked at me. "Don't worry, son, you're going to get in."

But I was worried.

I took Stuart out of my pocket and let him run up my arm as Charlie's eyes grew big. "Don't say anything," I whispered to her.

Day 1

CHAPTER 51

I took the call in my father's den. Even though he had moved out, the room still reeked of Harvard. I picked up a photo of my father and brother. It was taken at Jeffrey's high school graduation. Connor had photobombed them and was holding up four fingers, the Los Angeles Police Department's unofficial code for "it's cool."

Even though I was expecting the call, when the phone rang, I jumped. Kurt Boyle of Harvard Admissions called at precisely 4 p.m. "Hello, Higgs," he said in a friendly voice. He sounded young.

"Sir," I said, hitting the speaker button.

When I hung up the phone, I was starving. I stepped out of the office and felt great, like a weight had been lifted.

Dad was having a Chivas on the rocks in the living room. From the window, I could see my mother wandering around my garden.

"Well, what's the verdict?" my father asked. He was doing a lousy job of trying not to seem too concerned.

I didn't answer right away.

"Higgs?" my father said. He put his drink down.

"Dad," I began. I took a deep breath. "I'm not going to be a dentist, and I'm not going to Harvard."

I had thought that crushing my father's hopes and dreams would be exhilarating, but I was wrong. It felt rotten. As mad as I was at him for hurting Mom, I got no pleasure in seeing him in pain.

My father looked surprised, then sad. When did he get gray in his hair? Even though I was the one who'd been out all night and in jail, he was the one who looked drained.

"Higgs," Dad said, quickly composing himself. "There's something I need to say to you."

Okay. Here it comes, I thought. At last. I was actually glad he was going to chew me out. I braced for a bucketload of how I'd disappointed him. How I was nothing like Jeffrey and how I had let the entire family down. I was an impostor, the faux Jeffrey. I could never live up to his legacy. I had always been terrified that my father would figure out that truth.

"Higgs, I hope you're okay with not getting into Harvard," he said gently.

This was not what I was expecting.

"Are *you* okay with it?" I asked back.

Dad shrugged. "Clearly, Boyle didn't know what he was doing when he rescinded your offer, but I may be able to pull some strings. Dullaghan, our lawyer, has connections."

"Dad, I'm not going to Harvard," I said, this time more forcefully.

"You can reapply in the fall," he reassured me. "Higgs, it's okay. We'll get through this together."

Those were the words I had always longed to hear, only under different circumstances.

"Dad, I'm not going to Harvard."

"We'll lodge a formal protest, and in the meantime you can —"

"You're not listening to me!" I said raising my voice. "Harvard isn't for me, Dad!"

"Of course it is!" he said, sounding like his old self. "Higgs, you were born to be a Harvard man, it's your legacy! It's your dream."

He wasn't hearing anything I said. I spied Charlie eavesdropping in the hallway.

"Your mother isn't going to take this well," he said. "She's . . . she's got a lot on her mind."

"Yeah, like you moving out," I said bitterly.

My father's entire body tensed. "Maybe I've taken her for granted now and then, and maybe I haven't been home as much as she'd like, but she didn't have to kick me out of the house. That's insane. She's insane."

"What? Wait, it was Mom's idea for you to move out?"

Dad nodded. "I may have made some mistakes, and may not have been the best husband. But I can be. I can change," he insisted. "I just need a second chance."

What I would have given for one of those.

Day 1

CHAPTER 52

The shower felt great, like it was washing away layers of dirt and crud and lies and deceit that had built up over the years. I could have stayed in there forever.

"Higgs! Higgs?" Charlie was pounding on the bathroom door. "Mom says you've got two hours before the party and you should take a nap!"

I wasn't surprised that we were still going ahead with my graduation party. Why wouldn't we? It was four years in the making, and the only thing that kept my mother going. Plus, I may not have been going to Harvard, but I was still an alumnus of Sally Ride High School.

My lip was puffy, but it didn't look as bad as my black eye, which had acquired a deep purple hue. I took out my navy-blue debate suit from the closet and paired it with a light blue shirt and crimson tie. Crimson was Harvard's way of saying "red." It was their school color. It was the least I could do for my dad. He was having a really bad day.

Stuart was running around in my laundry basket. I scooped him up and put him in my pocket. Just then there was a knock on the door.

"Here," Charlie said. "This is for you."

"Thank you." I opened the box, thinking it was a graduation gift, and was surprised by what I saw.

"It's makeup," she said. "To cover your bruises and black eye. Most of it is Mom's. I figured that you may as well look good at your party. There are going to be lots of photos and stuff."

"Thank you, Charlie," I said. "I really mean that."

I thought I saw her blush.

The doorbell rang. It was Nick. "Ready?" he asked.

"Don't you think you should get some sleep?" Mom said, looking worried.

"There's stuff I have to do," I told her.

"Get him to the Carriage House restaurant by six forty-five p.m.," Dad instructed Nick. "The party starts at seven p.m. I don't want to give Higgs's mother any more reason to be upset. You know how women get."

I turned to my sister. "Charlie, want to go with us?"

"Really?" She broke into a stupid grin. "Hell, yeah!" Charlie said, jumping into the front seat. I stood next to the car until she got out and crawled into the back.

Nick hit the gas. "Where to?" he asked.

First stop: Sally Ride High School.

The parking lot that had been full just a couple hours earlier was empty — except for a rusted green Kia with a broken window.

I put an envelope on the front seat.

"What's in it?" Nick asked.

"Four hundred dollars," I said. For graduation, my (many) Chinese relatives had gifted me with red paper envelopes of cash. This was an ancient tradition that I wasn't about to argue against.

"You owed Mr. French four hundred dollars?" Charlie asked. "What, did you buy drugs from him or something?"

"Or something," I said.

There was no note in the envelope, but I knew that Mr. French would know who it was from.

At the next stop, I told Charlie and Nick to wait in the car. ". . . and keep the engine running," I instructed. "I may need to make a quick getaway."

I exhaled when no one answered the door. As I started back to the car I heard, "Higgs?"

I turned around.

"What do *you* want?" Roo said as she stood in the doorway framed by bouquets of flowers and balloons behind her.

"I want to tell you that I'm really, really sorry," I said — and I was. You don't go out with someone for two years, four months, and seven days and just forget about them. "I acted badly and I wish I could take it all back."

Roo looked pissed. "You were a poo," she said. "It was so embarrassing. All the other boyfriends said they'd give their girlfriends their kidneys. Higgs, you were a really big poo."

"Why don't you just go ahead and say that I was a shit," I told her. Rosemary "Roo" Wynn never cussed — it was one of her claims to fame. However, being called a poo didn't seem like the proper justice. "Go ahead," I goaded her. "Say it. I know you want to."

"Okay . . . Higgs, you were a . . ."

"Say it, Roo."

"You were a . . ."

"You can do it, Roo!"

"You were a . . . a . . . a shit. You were a shit! A shit! A shit! You're a shit!"

"Don't you feel better now?" I asked.

Roo caught her breath. She was flushed. "I do."

"So do you forgive me?" I asked. "No hard feelings, right?"

"I didn't say that, Higgs. I said you were a s-h-i-t. Now goodbye. Get out of my life."

"I'm not going to Harvard," I said, waiting to see her response.

"Where are you going?" she asked. "Hell?"

Roo slapped both hands over her mouth.

I had to laugh. "Come here," I said affectionately. Roo shook her head, hands still covering her mouth. "I love you," I said, laughing, and at that moment, I really did. "Come on, Roo. Two years, four months, and seven days."

We hugged, both knowing it would be for the last time.

Rosalee's house was only a block away, so I left Nick and Charlie in the car to continue their debate over the Beatles vs. the Clash. It looked like there was a party going on at the Gomez house. A backyard band was blasting. The side gate was open.

"Who invited you?" Rosalee asked. She was still wearing her graduation cap and gown, and was holding a plate of barbecue chicken wings.

"I'm sorry if I've hurt your feelings," I said, stepping away from the pool to be safe. With Rosalee, one never knew what she was capable of.

"You came here to tell me that?" she asked. Her eyes narrowed.

"Yes, and that I'm not going to Harvard."

Rosalee dropped the plate. Chicken wings scattered at my feet. A couple floated in the deep end of the pool, then sank.

"Someone snitched on me. Any idea who that might be?"

For once, Rosalee Gomez was speechless.

"I'm sorry, I'm sorry," she finally said. She was shaking. "I was so mad when you won the debate. Oh my god, I'm sorry."

"I'm not."

"Oh, crap, Higgs. I've ruined your life." Rosalee rushed me to a quiet corner of the backyard. "I didn't think they'd really do anything about it."

"Listen," I told her. "No hard feelings. I'm okay with this. Really. And Rosalee, I really am sorry. For everything."

"Higgs, I feel awful. I'm sorry. . . ."

"We're cool," I assured her. "I swear."

As I walked away, Rosalee called out, "Higgs? How did you know it was me?"

"I didn't," I said. "Until now."

"I refuse," Nick said as the three of us stared at the gravel pit. "I'm not crossing that."

"Me neither," Charlie added. "There are dead bodies in there."

"I promise, no one's going to get hurt."

Nick looked worried. Charlie looked uncertain. I held out my hand to my sister and she took it.

"Is this for real?" Charlie asked after we crossed and were marching through the woods. I'd been telling them about Monarch. "I mean, come on, Higgs. You just met this person with a ridiculous name who lives in a trailer, and you made a pact, and let a bunch of mice loose, and got beat up, and were stuck on the water tower, and are in love?"

"Don't make it sound cheap," I said.

When we neared the Airstream, I called out, "Monarch! Monarch!" I was anxious to get some answers. I knocked on the door. "Monarch?"

Charlie turned to Nick. "My brother's gone crazy, am I right?"

"Afraid so," Nick replied.

The door wasn't locked, so I took that as my invitation to step inside. My throat closed up when I looked around. The books were gone. The walls were bare. All traces of Monarch were gone. It was as if she had never existed.

Charlie pushed past me. "So this is the charming trailer you told us so much about."

We were about to leave, and that's when I spotted it in the corner on the floor — a candy-apple-red Zippo lighter with a rooster on it.

Day 1

CHAPTER 53

The parking lot was pretty full, but Nick snagged a spot next to a BMW. It was the same one I'd seen at the iffy Mart.

"Aren't you coming?" Charlie asked.

Nick was still sitting in the car, texting furiously.

"Come on, Nick," I said. "The party doesn't start until I arrive."

He shook his head. "I can't go," he said glumly. "Samantha's waiting for me. I'm already late."

"You can't expect me to go in there by myself, can you?" I said to him.

"I'm here," Charlie said.

Nick shrugged. "Higgs, you know how it is."

I nodded. I knew how it was.

I headed toward the party, then turned around. "Hey, Nick!" I called out. He stopped the car and rolled the window down. "Thank you."

"For what?"

"For doing so much research, for being there for me, for everything."

Outside the Carriage House restaurant, my father was on the phone, pacing.

"Of course we want to appeal," he was saying. He cupped his hand over the phone. "It's Dullaghan. We're going to make this right," he whispered.

"Have you heard nothing I've said?" I asked him.

"Higgs!" Mom came out and ushered me toward the Victorian room, where the graduation party was to take place. This was her one big splurge. She looked pretty in her pink dress and simple strand of pearls.

"Are you okay?" she asked.

I nodded. "More than you can imagine," I said honestly.

She exhaled. "Darling, I'm so glad." I gave her a long hug.

As my mother attended to a problem with irregular ice swans, I watched Charlie taking bites out of appetizers and then putting them back on the buffet.

"Do you hate me that much?" I asked.

Startled, Charlie choked on a cracker topped with smoked salmon and a smear of cream cheese.

"I know it was you," I said. "What I don't know is why."

"Why what?"

"Dinky Dick."

Charlie paled. "Who told you?"

"I saw the STartA logo on the back of the banner. That's your group, your art club or whatever."

"So?"

"Charlie, why would you do that to me?"

"It was a joke," she said defensively. "It all started as a joke."

"But why?"

"You were really mean to me, Higgs." Her gaze refused to meet mine. "I finally got fed up with it."

"How can you say I'm mean to you?" I asked. "I don't even talk to you."

"Precisely," Charlie said. "Our whole family is about you. Mom and Dad treat you like you're the center of the universe, and I'm just here, like an insignificant moon orbiting around the great Higgs Boson Bing.

"During our last STartA meeting, someone said that we should plaster the school with flyers, you know, as our final underground art project for the year."

"Your group did underground art projects? Like what?"

"Like when we covered Mr. Avis's car with aluminum foil."

"That was you guys?"

Charlie nodded proudly. "Yeah, that was us. But we wanted to do something bigger, that everyone would see. And I thought about those stupid flyers you were making for Senior of the Year and suggested we do a parody of them. You know, a social commentary on self-promotion and self-absorption."

Charlie exhaled and finally faced me. Her eyes were wet. "I swear, Higgs, I didn't mean for it to go as far as it did. I thought it would just be a couple of flyers that no one would really notice."

"Go on," I said.

"Then Abbie, she's the president of STartA, bribed some guy from the Dolby Sound Club to help her hack into the PA system. It started really getting out of hand when the others started

254

talking about the water tower assault. By the time I realized they were serious, it was too late. They recruited Libby Bukowski to paint the banner, and no one would listen to me when I begged them to stop. Honest, Higgs, I tried. They threatened to go to Kostantino and Avis and tell them it was all my idea. I could have gotten expelled."

Charlie leaned against the wall and then sank to the floor. "Higgs, do you hate me?"

"Do *you* hate *me*?" I said back to her. I took Stuart out of my pocket and let him sit on my shoulder.

"Sometimes," she admitted. "A lot of times," she added. "Okay, I do. I mean, I don't, but I do. Whatever."

"'Cause I'm a Dinky Dick?"

"Yeah, that and a thousand other reasons. Are you going to tell Mom and Dad?"

I shook my head. "No," I promised. "I won't say a word."

Charlie smiled. I had never noticed her smile before. It was like Mom's. "Can I ask you something?" she said.

"Anything."

"Why did you tell Boyle that you didn't want to go to Harvard?" Charlie asked.

I gave her a quizzical look.

"I was eavesdropping," she admitted. "From what I could hear, it sounded like they were still willing to take you."

My sister was right. They were willing to take me. I had outsmarted Harvard. Boyle had asked, "Did you or did you not create a fake animal advocacy group and solicit funds for it?"

"I did not," I answered truthfully.

In debate, if part of a statement is not true, it renders the entire statement invalid. Yes, I did create a fake animal advocacy group, but no, I did not solicit funds for it. Therefore, on a technicality, I was in the clear. "I did not create a fake animal advocacy group *and* solicit funds for it," I said.

"Great," Boyle had said.

"That's it?" I asked, surprised.

"We don't put much weight on anonymous calls," he explained. "So many kids would do anything to get into Harvard, even trying to eliminate those who are in so they can move up on the wait list."

"Mr. Boyle, sir," I told him. "Harvard is a great school. But I am rescinding my application. I won't be attending in the fall, or ever —"

Charlie was staring at me, waiting for an answer.

"Harvard was Dad's dream, not mine," I told my sister.

She shook her head, not understanding.

"I never wanted to be a dentist," I explained. "I just wanted to be like Jeffrey and make Dad happy. Now I'm sure he's going to be miserable."

"It wasn't me who told Harvard about SAP," Charlie said.

"I know," I assured her.

"Higgs?" Charlie asked. "If you end up staying at home 'cause you're not going to Harvard, can I still have Rolvo?"

Day 1

CHAPTER 54

The pair of ice swans looked regal, even if one was shorter than the other. It was a shame that they would eventually melt, and one of them would break its neck. Waiters and waitresses in black pants and crisp white shirts were standing at attention with their hands behind their backs, ready to attend to my guests' every need. A live band played Top 40 songs in a way that made them sound Bottom 10.

I was stationed by the door being reintroduced to my relatives, my mother's friends, and my father's colleagues as I let them and various other strangers hug me. My parents stood side by side, like strangers in an elevator. Both were smiling, although not at each other.

It was great to have Nick with me and no Samantha in sight. In a rare moment of assertiveness, he told her that he was coming to my party — with or without her. A handful of my friends from debate and track and band were at the bar trying to bribe the bartender to serve them beer.

After all the guests arrived and the mingling was under way, Dad pulled me out into the hallway. There was another big graduation party in the banquet room next door to ours and it was just as loud, if not louder. I looked through the doorway and spied an ice sculpture of the Eiffel Tower that was twice as tall as my swans.

"Don't tell anyone that your mother and I have separated," my father instructed. "And don't tell anyone you're not going to Harvard. If anyone asks, we'll just say you deferred admittance. There are lots of Harvard alums here and rumor has it that they'll be making me the chair of the Harvard Dental Alumni Association next year. That's big."

I went along with my father's request. After all, I realized that this was his party, not mine.

Dad looked over my shoulder and lit up. "Martin?" he cried out.

"Charles!" someone replied.

"Higgs, there's someone I want you to meet," my father told me, pushing me toward an imposing man wearing an expensive suit. "Martin," Dad said. "This is my son, Higgs. Higgs, this is Mr. Gowin."

"Ah, the Harvard man," Mr. Gowin said, shaking my hand. "Congratulations."

"What are you doing here?" Dad asked him.

"Same thing as you," he said, chuckling. "Spending too much money celebrating a high school graduation. Higgs, I want you to meet my daughter, Mindy. You two will be neighbors when you're at college. She's going to Tufts for prelaw, like everyone else in the family did."

Inside the banquet room next to mine was a girl standing with her back to us, near the Eiffel Tower.

"Mindy! Mindy, come here, there are some people I want you to meet," her father called out.

She turned around and we both froze.

"Mindy, may I have a word alone with you?" I said when I found my voice.

Day 1

CHAPTER 55

"*Mindy?*" I said. We were standing in the corridor near the restrooms. "Your name is Mindy?"

She was holding a plate filled with Swedish meatballs.

"Don't act so surprised, Higgs," she said. "It's unattractive."

"What happened to Monarch? Forgive me, but I am totally confused."

"Got a cigarette? I need a cigarette."

"You know I don't smoke," I snapped. "Can you please explain what's going on?"

"I was on a foreign exchange program in Paris," Monarch said with a weary sigh. "When I came home, there was still a week left of school, but I didn't think I could handle even one hour of Our Lady of the Holy Cross Excelsior Academy. . . ."

"So you lived in that trailer," I said, finishing her sentence.

Monarch nodded. "I went home most nights, or told my parents I was staying with friends."

That's when it hit me. "You drive a silver BMW, don't you?" I said.

Monarch nodded. "How did you know?"

"How did I not know?" I said rhetorically. "Please. Continue."

"Coming back was a shock to my system. In Paris, I had freedom. My host family really didn't care what I did. They never made me check in with them or anything. I loved it. Here, I had my entire life planned out since birth."

"I know the feeling," I said. "But why weren't you straight up with me? Why did you lie? Was it fun stringing me along? Making me look stupid? You played me the entire time."

"I never told you anything you didn't want to hear," Monarch said defensively. "You ate up everything I said about living in the woods. If you were really paying attention, Mr. Debater, you could have torn my story to shreds — but you believed what you wanted to believe."

"You lied to me," I said bitterly.

Monarch tensed. "You lied to yourself, Higgs."

I was so pissed at her. The air between us was thick. Every now and then someone would call out, "Hey Higgs!" or "Hi Mindy!!!"

Neither of us responded. We were too busy glaring at each other.

"So, correct me if I am wrong," I said, "but your real name is Mindy Gowin and you will be attending Tufts in the fall, and then you'll be on your way to Yale Law School, if all goes according to plan?"

"What's it to you?" she asked. "Besides, you're going to Harvard."

"No I'm not," I told her.

"Oh, Higgs," Monarch said, her voice catching. She reached for my hand. "I'm so sorry."

"I'm not," I said, pulling away from her. "I turned them down. Ironic, isn't it? You're the Ivy League bullshitter. Being a Dinky Dick is nothing compared to how foolish you've made me look. I hope you had fun."

"I did," Monarch said, sounding serious. "Didn't you?"

"You turned my life upside down."

"Answer the question," Monarch said forcefully. "Did you have fun?"

I was about to give her three arguments as to how she ruined my life. In debate, you never let them back you into a corner. When the opposition blasts you with questions, the best defense is to rephrase the question to throw them off, never directly answering or giving anything away.

"Did you have fun?" she pressed.

Despite my greatest efforts, a smile threatened to appear.

"Yes," I admitted.

"Thought so," she said triumphantly.

Monarch's face was scrubbed clean. There was no black around her eyes or red on her lips. Even the butterfly tattoo on her shoulder was missing. The only thing I recognized was the diamond "M" necklace — the one she said she pawned.

Just then, someone yelled, "Mindy!"

A guy who looked like he was ripped from the pages of a fashion magazine was barreling toward us.

"Jack," Monarch said, looking flustered. "You're here."

"I wanted to surprise you," he said, flashing perfect teeth. I ran my tongue over my chipped tooth. He picked Monarch up and gave her a long hug, then looked at me glaring at him.

When I didn't say anything, Monarch made the introductions. "Jack, this is Higgs. Higgs, this is Jack. Jack goes to Yale," she said, as if that would explain everything.

"How do you know my girlfriend?" Jack asked without taking his eyes off of Monarch.

I felt like I had just been punched by the twins.

"We . . . we . . . ," she began.

"It's a funny story," I said. Monarch started to interrupt me, but I wouldn't let her. "You're not going to believe this, but we met on a student exchange program. In Paris."

Monarch gave me an almost imperceptible smile. I held up my finger, the one that we had made our blood pact with, and waved it at her.

"That's nice," Jack said, clearly more interested in her than me. "France is a great place to study. I went to Japan my senior year of high school."

He kissed her and I winced. "Cupcake," he said. "I'm gonna go get a drink and say hi to your parents."

When Jack accidentally walked into my grad party, not hers, neither Monarch nor I tried to stop him.

"Cupcake?" I said, mimicking his voice. "You're going out with someone who calls you Cupcake?"

Monarch shrugged. "You're one to criticize. Your name is Higgs Boson, you have a sister named Charlie, and you dated a person named Roo."

Touché.

"So, what's his deal? What's his major — being an asshole?"

"Do you mean 'dinky dick'?" she teased. "Actually, Jack's a nice guy."

"He's not the right guy for you," I told her. "Anyone can see that. Plus, would he have bled for you like I did?" I pointed to my eye.

Monarch studied my face. "Are you wearing makeup?"

"I'm doing a lot of things these days that I didn't used to do. So then, were you just slumming it with me?"

"Au contraire," she answered. "I believe it was you who was slumming it with me." Monarch looked toward the banquet room. "What I would give for a cigarette."

"Cigarettes will kill you."

"Everyone in Paris smokes," Monarch said. "That's where I picked it up."

"We're not in Paris now," I reminded her.

"We should be," she said wistfully.

I took a step toward her, and she didn't back away. "When I told you that I loved you, you never did tell me if you felt the same way," I said. "Do you?"

"Is that your bonus question?"

"Yes, that's my bonus question."

Monarch hesitated, and instead of her usual snappy reply, said, "You don't fit into my plans, Higgs. Living in the woods, being a rebel, that was all a sideline, like an elective or summer school or something. It was my own *Roman Holiday*. But now I have to get on with my real life. I mean, maybe if you were going to Harvard, we could have —"

I nodded. I got my answer. She loved me, but she just didn't know it yet. "You don't need to say anything more," I told her.

"So what will you do?" Monarch asked.

I shrugged. "I really don't know. I hear Cornell has a great agricultural school. Maybe I can apply in the fall."

"Farmer Higgs," she mused.

"It wouldn't be so bad," I answered. "Do you think you could ever love a farmer?"

There was an awkward silence.

"Well then, I suppose we both should probably get back to our guests and our real lives," Monarch said.

I watched her walk away.

"Wait!" I said, sprinting after her. "I have something for you — a graduation gift." I reached into my pocket. Stuart was in there with her cigarette lighter.

"Seriously, Higgs?" Monarch asked as I opened up my hand.

"Seriously."

Just then, Charlie came running up to me. She glanced at Monarch. "Higgs, Mom says to come back. Everyone's asking for you."

"I'll be right there," I said. I turned to Monarch and extended my hand. "It was nice getting to know you," I said. "I mean that."

She shook my hand. "Likewise, Higgs Boson Bing. I predict great things for you."

"Was that her?" Charlie asked as we headed into my party.

"Yeah, that's her," I said.

"She doesn't look anything like you described. And I can't believe you gave her your mouse."

My mother was talking with guests. "I've decided to go back to work," I heard her say. She looked happier than I had seen her in a long time.

"Harvard!" one of my father's cronies called out, raising a glass to me. "Veritas!"

"Veritas" was the school's motto. It meant truth.

Dad was standing by the bar with his college buddies, watching me.

"Harvard!" the man said again. In unison, all the Harvard alums raised their glasses to me.

Someone placed a glass of champagne in my hand. I stared at my father before lifting my glass. "Veritas!" I called out, giving him a chipped-tooth smile.

Today would be for my father, I had decided. But tomorrow would be for me.

ACKNOWLEDGMENTS

I would like to thank my editor, Arthur Levine, and my agent, Jodi Reamer, plus Nick Thomas, who, along with Cheryl Klein and Elizabeth Parisi, helped bring this book to life. Special thanks to Oliver Valcorza, Doug Gettinger, and Will Hermes for answering my many questions. To my friends — Henry Gowin, Dan Santat, Jeannie Birdsall, and my Third Act compatriots, I am grateful for your continual support. To Mom, Dad, and Benny, I couldn't have done it without you. And finally, to Kait, who climbed the water tower and lived to tell about it — I love you, but don't ever do that again.